SUITS AND SKINS

Taming the CEO

DJ Gunn

Vision to Keys Publishing

ISBN-13: 9798991477406

Cover design by: Vision to Keys
Library of Congress Control Number: 2018675309
Printed in the United States of America

To Deven and Roddy,

*Thanks for reminding me that life is about the
laughter between the nuances of living.*

CONTENTS

CHAPTER 1 – GAVIN BRIGHT

In times like this, I wonder why I adopted Kevin. My frustration level is high, like Defcon level 2, the code we used for my old platoon when there was a threat of losing many lives, like a nuclear disaster-level threat. And yet, after all the training and all the missions, I have allowed Kevin to get under my skin and create a sense of uneasiness.

It's been almost four months since I permitted Kevin to stay, but his persistent whining about leaving home at night wore me down, so I made a cat door for him. Kevin can come and go as he pleases; I didn't imagine he would have returned with so-called presents for me the following day.

Kevin likes to return in the wee hours of the morning, bearing gifts that he would present to me. I believe, in some weird way, he is grateful that I took him in from the mean streets and wants to award me with presents. However, it is concerning that he is placing these odd things on my bed.

The first time, he brought back some sort of silk head covering. After further investigation, I discovered that African American women wore them to protect their hair when they went to bed. It's also called a bonnet, but it is not like the ones my mother and aunt wore to church on Easter.

My buddy Alex could ease my mind the last time Kevin left something on my bed.

Alexander Donnelly, who served in the Marine Special Forces with me and is now my business partner, convinced me that when Kevin left women's pantyhose on my bed, he was just dumpster diving. However, the pantyhose had a clean scent—not that I sniffed them or anything like that. They smelled and looked clean.

Kevin has brought socks, hair ties, and candy wrappers home throughout the months. However, this is the final straw.

Dialing my good friend for over a decade to pull me from the ledge, I scream into the phone when he answers on the first ring.

"This is too much this time, Alex. Kevin left a tiny pink polka-dot bikini bottom, and I do not know where it's been."

Alex's boisterous laughter is so loud that I have to adjust the volume on my cell phone.

"I swear," Alex explains, "It seems like Kevin has been to some exciting places. Maybe I should adopt your cat."

"You know I do not mind bikinis, remember Cancun?"

"Awe, yes, Cancun, good times."

"Yeah, I like seeing bikinis attached to beautiful

bodies, but not randomly on my...I am careful about things placed on my bed. My bed is my sanctuary, Alex."

Alex continues laughing in my ear. Between his laughter, he starts to form sentences.

"After all we have been through, like the Crandaghi Mission, you are one of the toughest motherfuckers– one of the toughest Marines in the squad. The missions, the rescues, and the women, but somehow, a little stray cat has you on edge."

"Kevin is far from being little," I sigh. Kevin is a big striped Tabby cat, so big that I didn't believe he was a stray at first, but I took him in after he cried at my door every night for a week straight. "He is a bit odd but never *little*."

I look down at Kevin, who stares back at me while lying on my Persian rug. The bright orange color of his fur matches the expensive wool carpet. He tries to give me a charming look, but his features can't pull it off. Frankly, he is not attractive. His left eye is more significant than the right, and his meows sound like he smokes due to the husky, ugly tone he makes.

"Gavin," Alex chuckles. "It is going to be okay. Don't make me remind you I warned you not to take him in with your condition," he laughs even more.

"What condition?" I snarl.

"Your OCD, you know, man. Even your cleaning lady has a cleaning lady."

I shake my head. "You're no help."

"No help? I offered to take him off your hands if you take the Danvers Research Lab case."

Alex is a partner with a minority stake in my private security company. With the unique skill sets we developed in the Marine Corps, we wanted to continue the discipline, leadership, and sense of duty we cultivated over the years to create a successful business where former military personnel can fulfill their passions and earn a living.

Since there is a growing demand for investigative and security services in various sectors, we fill this need with our experienced team to ensure high service standards. We currently have over 500 employees. We protect companies' assets and provide private details for celebrities. However, our specialty is making complex problems disappear.

Alex signed the Danvers Research Lab contract several weeks ago when I was wrapping up a security gig in New Mexico. Since then, he has been trying to convince me to lead the team in overseeing the security protocols for her company and protecting the scientists who are apparently receiving random threats.

"I would rather do another mission in Uzbekistan than be near a lab, much less inside one; you should know that," I yell towards the phone that I put on speaker near the tiny bikini while putting on my gray joggers. "Besides, Smitty said the owner is a piece of work."

"She is demanding, that's all. Her scientists have been getting threats about working for her research center, and they are escalating." His voice falters, and he hesitates as if grappling with the decision to continue speaking.

"Spit it out, man; why would you think I would ever take the lead for a company that does work with research and labs?" I shout out.

Alex continues, never mincing words. "It is not like a regular experimental lab, or I wouldn't have asked. You don't even have to go inside the research area. The building has spaces that are compartmentalized into different sectors with offices, executive suites, and, you know, high-end stuff."

Do I need to remind him about the last time I was in a lab, what they did to me, what they did to our fellow marine, who we call our brother?

"I am sorry, man," Alex says, breaking me out of my thoughts. "I didn't forget. I thought it would be good for you. No worries, Smitten has it."

Kevin starts meowing loudly before I can answer Alex, indicating it is time for me to feed him.

"Good God, he doesn't seem to be getting better. What did the vet say?" Alex questions, his voice laced with concern.

"He said that was his cat voice. He is hungry and reminding me it's feeding time." I continue and calm down tensions. "Smitty is a good choice to take point on the lab job. I will take point on the Sci-Fi convention next week in D.C. Besides, the only Ms. Danvers I heard of was a fictional character in Rebecca, and because of that book, the name Danvers gives me the creeps."

"Rebecca? Man, is there a book you haven't read?"

I grin, "Literature is not a bad thing. You have computers, and I have my books."

"Okay," he agrees. "Duncan and I will be coming over to discuss the status of the recently signed contracts."

Duncan is another one of my best friends. Like brothers in arms, we served together and now work together. However, Duncan is a wild card. He likes the thrill and the action the job provides but doesn't want to be a partner. He likes his freedom.

"I have everything ready in the office; I can help troubleshoot the Danvers' case. I have some ideas and am glad to offer surveillance and support outside the facility. We can shoot some pool and talk about the new hires and where we are with establishing protocols."

"Copy, see ya." Alex ends the call.

Kevin's loud meow echoes throughout the house. I decided to finish getting dressed later and head down the spiral staircase. "Coming, Kevin, hold on!"

A ringing chime breaks me out of my feeding ritual as I pour Kevin's favorite cat food into his bowl.

Is that my doorbell? I thought. *It couldn't be Alex and Duncan so soon. Besides, they have the code for the keyless entry pad.* I would ignore it on an early Sunday morning. It is most likely a solicitor or Mormon with a sales pitch. *Everyone these days has a sales pitch.*

Yeah, ignoring the doorbell is the best course of action.

I glance down at my attire and notice I am only wearing my gray joggers. I was coming out of the shower when I spotted the tiny pink polka dot bikini on my bed.

Continuing my routine, I pick up Kevin's water bowl and ease it into the sink to clean and fill it.

"Fuck," I say out loud in the air when the loud chime sounds again.

This person will not stop ringing my bell. Okay, buddy. It so happens that I have cameras all around the perimeter of my home, and the footage feeds into the app on my cell phone.

Scanning around the room for my cell phone to see if I could pick up the action on my surveillance camera, I realize I left it on my bed. Annoyance rages through my body. This is a Defcon level 3 threat.

Should I go to the lower level to observe my state-of-the-art surveillance cameras in real-time? No, I live in one of the most upscale gated communities in Loudon County, Virginia, which means this obnoxious person can access my community.

Trekking through the foyer, I feel the cold marble floor on my bare feet, which will definitely need to be mopped to remove the smudges on the shimmering surface. *I didn't have time to put on socks. I am at Defcon level 2.* I grimace as I reach to open the door.

"What is so damn important that you want to break my doorbell?" I bellow, my anger clouding my vision, not even seeing who the entitled person was.

"What kind of sicko trains Trixie to come to my

house at night, take my things, then leave during the day to take them back to you?" The loud yet melodic voice bellows back.

"Huh?" I question the person at the door.

The vision startles me. At my door stood a young, no more than twenty-five, beautiful Black woman wearing a mean expression to match her worn Yankees oversized T-shirt and what looked like bicycle shorts with fuzzy pink house slippers.

Her curly, long, dark hair stood high on her head, barely held in place by one of those hair clips Kevin had brought home several times. Damn, her features are genuinely one-of-a-kind and uniquely stunning. *Shit, she is beautiful.* My breath catches a hitch when those warm brown eyes meet mine.

If she is not a Siren, my name is not Gavin Bright.

She continues speaking, and I must slow my breathing to listen to what she is saying.

"I adopted Trixie two months ago. I took him to the vet, and he comes to visit me after midnight when I arrive home, then he runs back to your house in the wee hours of the morning with *my* stuff," the Siren exclaims.

Her eyes wander up and down my nude tattooed torso, and I notice her stare linger a bit at my nipple piercings. When our eyes meet, I spot a hint of embarrassment on her face, which gives me great satisfaction.

"Trixie?" I ask, trying to contain my chuckle.

"Yeah, the big orange tabby," she cocks her head to the side to indicate that I should already know what she was referring to, but I was only focusing on her round pouting lips.

"It seems there is some misunderstanding. *Kevin* is my cat," I say to the Siren, relaxing my voice not to let her know the effect she has on me.

Her story makes little sense. Kevin has been bringing me stuff over the last two months. Could this be the owner of the purple lipstick, bracelets, hair bows, and many other obtuse items, the latest being a tiny bikini bottom? Hmm, maybe if she turns around, I will measure the size of her rear end to compare.

"*Your* cat?" she says, waking me from my speculations.

Her eyes dart back and forth to the road as if looking out for someone.

"Are you going to let me stay in your doorway all day so the entire neighborhood can hear us, or give me back my items so I can go?" She huffs.

"My apologies. Please come in." I step aside, and to my surprise, she enters my house like she owns the place. As she steers past me, I get a whiff of her scent or perfume, which is familiar, like the honeysuckle flowers in my hometown of Beeville, Kentucky.

She sashays into my foyer, calling, "Trixie darling. Come here. The gig is up. Where are my things?"

The traitor Kevin came out, licking his mouth of the food he had just devoured. He looks over to me, then her, and flops down in front of her fluffy pink slippers for a belly rub.

She then turns around and whispers in a menacing, told-you-so voice, "See?"

I release a chuckle. *See? All I can see is that ass in those bike shorts and not a panty line in sight. Did Kevin steal her panties, too?* I smile at the thought.

She bends over again to pet Kevin, and my cock jerks in my pants. The sun radiates on her rich brown, long, toned legs through the lined palladium windows.

"What kind of name is Trixie for a large male cat?" I ask while covering my crotch area with the community newsletter magazine that I brought in from outside.

Thank the gods that it was a thick issue.

She looks back and up at me as she squats down deeper and rubs Kevin some more.

"I didn't know it was a male cat when he came to me initially, but when I had time to take him to the vet near my work, I found out she was a *he*."

She rubs Kevin's belly, and his purrs fill the room. "Isn't that right, my big boy?" she coos in a playful voice.

I wish she were rubbing me like that.

"After you found out he was a male cat, why do you still call him Trixie?" I ask because maybe I am curious or a methodical, logical person who cannot see any reason for naming an irritable and temperamental cat like Kevin a girlie name like Trixie.

She stands up to her full height, a foot shorter than my 6'5 stature. Her house slippers make a tapping sound on my marble floors as she walks towards me.

The Siren is causing my heart to patter faster. I put my hand at my side, my fingers making a tight fist, and I am sure I am no longer inhaling and exhaling breaths.

She stops short of closing the distance between us to look at the floor-to-ceiling palladium windows I designed. When I remodeled the house, I found a solution for the contractor's problems by getting approval from the county and the Homeowners Association.

Her eyes went to my pristine quartz marble mosaic tiles, then discretely to the leather board-and-batten accent wall leading to the dining room.

"This is nice, fancy," she exaggerates the word fancy and continues to rate the aesthetics of my home. "And super clean." She folds her arms across her hole-infested Yankee T-shirt, a style I wouldn't wear even as a teenager, and exaggerates her words. "Wow, these are beautiful, upgraded features. Very nice indeed."

Her gaze then went over to my chest, then slowly down to see what I was holding in front of my crotch area. Her left eyebrow inquisitively rises as she eyes me with suspicion.

"It's the latest issue." I glance at the magazine, "I couldn't wait to read the Summer's Spring Ridge Club Pulse; it was outside the door." I smile and say, "Just stay put for one second while I grab a shirt." I see her arch her brow, and I add. "Please."

I ran up the stairs, taking two stairs at a time, quickly changing into jeans and a T-shirt. It did not even take a full minute to get back downstairs.

Of course, she defied me and didn't stay put.

She is now sitting on one of my Wilson Emmet designer bar stools, her elbows propped up on my Calcutta quartz counter, which picks up fingerprints just as quickly as Kevin picks up random items.

I will have to wipe the counter clean after she leaves. Fingerprints belong at a booking station in a perps file, not on my Calcutta counter. Alex is right; even my cleaning lady has a cleaning lady. OCD is real.

"Since you *moved?*" I turn to face her on the other side of the giant quart slab, picking up a coaster to place down. "May I offer you a coffee or tea?" I ask, but my voice trails off. I say in a low whisper, "Since you decided to sit at the counter."

"You may," she responds with a whimsical smile.

She short-circuited my brain with that snarky answer after thinking for one long second. I decide to be polite again.

"*Would* you like a cup of coffee or tea?"

She looks up at the ceiling, tilts her head to the side, and a sinister smirk appears.

"Coffee contains caffeine, and caffeine is a stimulant. Said stimulant fires up your brain and takes you from a regular mood to a go-go-go-you-can-do-it mood to get you through your day." She uses her hands like a cheerleader and raises one fist when she says the words go.

I didn't think she could short-circuit my brain again. I stare at her, wondering what she is going on about.

She continues. "On the other hand, tea is for the complicated soul; it doesn't have the super punch that caffeine holds, but it has its own superpowers."

Cupping her hand over the right side of her mouth, she mimics the international hand sign for telling a secret and leans in over the counter. "Tea contains an amino acid called L-theanine, which promotes relaxation and peace. Hmm, do I want to relax, or do I want to crank this up a bit?" She tilts her head at an angle as if in deep thought.

"Are you trying to be funny or rude?" I am Defcon level 4 annoyed because my counter has smudges. "Tea, coffee, or the door?" I snap back.

"Now, *who is* being rude?" She hisses.

She swivels around the bar stool and puts her whole hands, *both of them,* on the counter to stop. I am now Defcon level 3 annoyed.

"Neither," she states as she hops off the stool and puts her hands on the counter again like she knew I had a problem with the streaks and fingerprints.

Her movie-star-looking face and gorgeous brown eyes stare contemptuously as she points at me.

"I want my things, *everything* that Trixie brought

to you. I saw him take my swimsuit bottoms on a spy camera I recently set up at the house. I knew something was off; I'm missing hair ties, socks, and other small items," her voice went low; I believe she didn't want to elaborate on the small items. "If you can't find everything now, give me the bottom of my swimsuit; it is part of a set. I need it for today's community pool party."

"Is that the neighborhood pool party that's taking place this evening?" I ask while wetting a paper towel to clean the counter. "Don't you have to be an owner to attend?"

Her glare grows, adequately explaining the phrase: *If looks could kill.*

"Why don't you think I am a homeowner? Trixie is taking *my* things out of *my* house." She folds her arms across her chest. "What, because I am Black, you think I can't afford to purchase a home in Spring Ridge Club? Or maybe you think I am the help," she snarls.

My hand rises in protest. "No, because you are young and pretty, and only older people live in this community. The latest edition of the Spring Ridge Pulse states that no guests or children of the owners can attend the pool party."

"So, you think I am someone's *child?*" She squints her eyes. "Because I can't possibly earn enough to live in this exclusive gated community. I live three houses away from you. You are a self-absorbed narcissist who assumes that a Black woman must either rent, stay with a friend, or be an adopted child of a rich family to live here." She sighs. "I am north of thirty years old, if you must know."

My eyes widen. If my old platoon could see how she just ripped into me, I would be teased at every get-together for as long as we had get-togethers. Her words cut me to the core, even though this is not the first time I've been called a narcissist.

"I didn't mean to insult you. It's that you don't fit the makeup of the type of folks that live here," I reply.

Shit, I just put my foot in my mouth again; the makeup of the type of folks that live here? I needed to clean it up and tell her how young she looked.

"North of thirty?" I raise my right eyebrow. "You, you look a lot younger..."

She cut me off before I could tell her that she could pass for a teen. "Well, what about you? You look like you're twelve." She unfolds her hands, but I notice her hands curl into fists. "Why can you own a home here and not me?"

"Well, I'm not twelve. I am thirty-three, and yeah, good point," I say with a grin, hoping she won't spank me, or maybe secretly hoping she would.

She is about a foot shorter than me, and I outweigh her by around 100 pounds. Here I am, a striking 6'5" and 235 pounds. I know I convey power and confidence with my imposing physique, but the ladies always seem captivated by my charm. Not her, though, not her. She is not even intimidated by me at all; she intimidates me.

"I'll get your pink polka-dot bikini," I say with a nervous chuckle as I run up the steps again.

It took me 30 seconds to grab the bikini bottom.

As I hand it to her, she nods with a wry smile, "Oh, don't worry, it fits me just fine." She snatches it from my hold and heads toward the foyer.

Her hips sway to the beat the slippers made on my tile.

"Goodbye, Trixie, wherever you are hiding." She turns back to say one last thing. "Good day, Mr. Bright. Although there was nothing *Bright*," she makes air quotes, "about our meeting."

She closes the door, leaving my jaw and my masculinity on the floor. *She knows my last name, but how?* I run to the foyer to peer out the window just in time to see her disappear past the decorated fern trees in the front yard.

I quickly retrieve the latest addition to the Community Newspaper to confirm the time of the pool party.

A lazy Sunday will still occur, but I won't review all our case files. I will attend my first pool party in five years of living here.

CHAPTER 2 – DEIDRA DANVERS

"He is absolutely the opposite of Bright," I whisper to Carol Reynolds, my fifty-five-year-old neighbor, as she sways her feet back and forth in the pool while sitting on the pool deck.

Carol's floppy hat protects her from the sun's rays as she looks down at me. Her expression is expressionless, but I remember she said her Botox was finally kicking in since she got it done last week.

"It can't be that bad, Deidra," she says, leaning closer to hear the juicy gossip. "So, you don't think you can secure his vote?"

I swim to the other end, grab the railing, and pull myself out to chat with Carol again. I feel eyes on me, and I am grateful I wore boy shorts over the little polka-dot bikini.

Wearing a tiny bikini wouldn't bode well for a candidate running to be the HOA President and trying to earn votes to get on the Homeowners' Association board.

"I don't want his vote," I reply as we move our lounge chairs out of the sun to the sizeable brown umbrella. I add, "Mr. Cambel just left, and he promised to put a good word in for me with the other members at

Pickleball."

Mr. Cambel is a highly respected fixture in the community. When he said his goodbyes thirty minutes ago, the seventy-five-year-old retired astronaut gladly informed me he would be happy to campaign on my behalf. I am confident I will receive his vote. I smile at the thought.

"Are you sure about Mr. Bright though? The women here are enamored by him. He is very polite and charming, and those eyes." Carol sips her lemonade and continues, "Did you see those eyes? Are you sure he is a pervert?"

Her comment takes me aback. "Please don't call him a pervert. I just said *that I believe* he trained Trixie to take my things to his house." I lean back in the chair and fold my arms.

"He does have gorgeous eyes, though," I agree. I recall those sexy silver orbs peering down at me, and I am taken aback again at the way my lady parts get excited.

"Geez, I wouldn't mind if that cat of yours took *my* things to his house," Carol admits while fanning herself. "I would make sure to give him a go."

We started snickering.

Carol let out a deep sigh. "I am glad a young woman like you came to this boring community to spice things up. We have young people, mostly college kids or children, who came back to live with their parents, but you own your own home here. How long has it been, Diedra?"

"Since I moved in? Only three months," I respond.

I don't share with Carol that I was only attracted to the community because I was impressed with the security and gates keeping people who didn't own a home here out. Since the threats that the company has been receiving ramped up to include direct threats at me, I needed to find a place where I felt safe.

Coffee, tea, or the door.

While swimming earlier, his rude comment played in my mind, and his words drowned out Carol's voice as she continued to gossip about the neighborhood.

He is an asshole. A tattooed, nipple pierced - both, muscles upon muscles with the imprint of his cock in the gray sweatpants, hot and sexy kind of asshole. Those silver eyes, dark wavey hair, and full, luscious lips are why women around here swoon. I know I am wrong for accusing him of training Trixie to take my things and calling him a narcissist, but he was mean to me first.

"You are so deep in thought," Carol laughs, taking me out of my deep thoughts as she states.

"Huh, what did you say?" I pull down my sunglasses, doing the weird thing that wired individuals do to enhance their focus, like turning down the music to concentrate on seeing the road.

"I *said*, you have been in the community for only three months and just going over to see Spring Ridge Club's most eligible bachelor."

"Eligible bachelor?" I raise an eyebrow.

"The community comprises of married couples, widows, widowers, and families with mostly college kids, which we often put in the guest's home. It's rare for folks like Mr. Bright to live here." Carol continues, "Fiona just returned from Cambridge and has him in her sights."

"Whose Fiona?" I huff while sitting up in the seat to hear more. *Why do I care?*

"She is the accomplished daughter of the Johnstone family, the house up from the clubhouse."

"You mean the estate that guest house looks like my main house?"

"That's the one." She smirks while putting on sunscreen. "I know Fiona is probably stewing that the invites were only for the homeowners."

"I already received Johnstone's vote," I whisper with glee. "Last month, I met Esmeralda Johnstone by the pool, and we hit it off. She promised to share her interior designers with me to get me started." I sigh. "I don't know what to do with my living room. It's so big."

"Wait, you got the Johnstone's vote?" Carol asks with wide eyes.

I give Carol a lazy smile, ready to spill the gossip. "Esmeralda told me about the feud her dearest husband is having with the current HOA Board, and she said she will convince her husband to vote for me. We exchanged numbers. We talk almost every day now."

"On a first-name basis? You move fast. She hasn't spoken to me in all my years of living here. I guess she doesn't talk with us old geezers." Carol smiles and tries to hide her hurt feelings.

"Well, if she doesn't talk to old geezers, she should have spoken to you because you are no old goozer, geezer, or whatever else you try to call yourself."

"You are so kind, darling," she murmurs.

"You are too awesome to be a geezer," I blush at my charming, valid words, "And Esmeralda is not like that. At first, she is shy and suspects people around here are judging her because she is Mr. Johnstone's second wife and with her being 24 years his junior. I will introduce you to her." I place my hand on top of hers.

"You ladies aren't going to swim?" An unfamiliar voice interrupts our conversation.

"Oh, Phil, what a surprise. It is a rare treat to see you at these events." Carol exits her lounge chair, maneuvering out of the flimsy chair to stand. Phil reaches in to hold her hand to stabilize her footing.

"Deidra, I would like to introduce you to Phillip Mullins, the President of Spring Ridge HOA and Country Club."

Phillip puts his feet together and bows abruptly, causing me to chuckle and be amused at the effort.

"At your service," Phil gloats. "It is wonderful to find beauty so rare to bless our presence at Spring Ridge, even though this is an owner's only pool event." He turns and winks at Carol. "I won't say anything, Carol. Any guests of yours are welcome." He attempts to whisper, but I can tell that some members near us ears start perking up. Or maybe this guy is doing this for the show.

I stand up out of the chair.

"Thank you for your compliment, but not at the expense of the beautiful souls who have shown me so much welcoming warmth since I moved into this community." I want to continue, but Phil interrupts me. A small crowd gathers around us to hear the lazy commotion.

"Ridiculous child, the only welcome packet I have signed was for the Danvers family that moved in around three months ago," he chuffs. "Carol, where did this person come from?"

The crowd grows.

"Phil, meet Deidra Danvers, CEO of the soon-to-be publicly traded Danvers Laboratories and Research Center, the new club member, and the candidate for *your* seat on the HOA Board."

I hear Phil gasp as his face turns a bright shade of red.

Perfect timing. I give Carol a knowing smile as more homeowners gather and applaud Carol's announcement. I smile and wave to the audience. This is the moment when I tell them why I want to become a Spring Ridge HOA board member.

I am eloquent with my words. I am brave and intelligent, and I won't let this pompous ass put me down.

I start wielding a tale about the beautiful community and how it can become greater...

CHAPTER 3 – GAVIN

"Just take the shot, already." I bellow at my colleague and best buddy, Alex while glancing at my watch. My impatience grew by the literal minute.

The guys reviewed the three complicated new contracts signed in one week. All of them are lucrative and have the potential for more business. One in particular, the Danvers case, started preliminary planning over the last few weeks.

To get a head start, I had them come over to discuss who was taking the lead on the critical cases since our new hires are still undergoing a strict probationary period. Out of the eleven cases we signed over the last couple of weeks, these three are complicated. For some, like the Danvers, we had to take measures immediately due to safety concerns.

"Dude, you were the one who insisted we come over for barbecue and beer, and now you are rushing us," Alex says, chalking his cue again.

"Because he has a hot date," Duncan snaps, sprawling on the couch, sipping his beer, and waiting for his turn for me to beat his ass in pool.

"Not a date." I bit the hot dog and spit out the bite

in a napkin since it was cold, we finished grilling hours ago. "It's a new neighbor that I want to see."

"Oh, the one you mentioned earlier about Kevin bringing her stuff to you," Alex comments, taking the shot and smiling as the five ball went into the pocket he called out.

"Is she hot?" Duncan chimes in while shuffling on his feet to stand up, more alert.

"*Is she hot?*" I mock him, sticking out my tongue. "What are you twelve?" That statement instantly made me think about the neighbor's ass in the bicycle shorts and what she said to me earlier.

"You are going to dump us for some new neighbor chick?" Duncan continues. "Hurrying us up like we work for you." He scratches his head. "Okay, technically, I *do* work for you, but we have history." He reaches to wrap his large hand around my shoulder, but I duck.

I shoot him a knowing nod. We do have history. I met Duncan in the Marine Corps. Special Forces. Benjamin Duncan stayed in for one more tour, but Alex and I wanted out. Duncan craves the chase of a mission; he is one of our best point men. Most people refer to him by his last name because Benjamin does not fit his brutal exterior. He is one inch over me in height, and he boasts he can take me, but he never did and won't dare to try.

"I agree. You can't erase history," Alex says, pointing to his chest, gesturing at the nipple piercings under his shirt. We all got them years ago to symbolize our warrior spirit. He frowns and scans our eyes. "Well, I still have mine."

"I kept mine in, too." Duncan's face holds a sly grin. "My ladies will be so disappointed if I *remove* our *history*."

My thoughts immediately took me to the time after we completed one of our most complicated missions. We went to a back alley tattoo parlor hidden in an alley in a border town near the northern border of Guatemala and Belize.

We all decided to get the piercings after Cortez, a revered member and one of my closest friends in the Special Forces Recon team, FORECON, hounded us to get them.

Five of us crowded into a small tattoo parlor. We vowed only to tattoo our MOS, military occupational specialty code 0321, marking our exceptional achievement in the United States Marine Corps. Specifically, it represents Marines in reconnaissance, Recon.

All four of us not only left with the code 0321 on the inside of our left biceps but also with the nipple piercings.

"Roman soldiers, the elite ones, received piercings to signify their strength and fortitude," Cortez dared us, and the tattoo artist nodded his head in agreement while focusing on completing the last of Alex's tattoos.

Duncan's eyes widened; he was the first to rip off his shirt. "Fire them up."

I smile, recalling the event.

"You are up, Mr. Sunshine," Alex says, bringing me out of my thoughts. He then takes the beer from my hand

and hands me my cue stick.

I lean across the table to take a wide-angle shot, ignoring Alex's and Duncan's Oohs and Awes, pretending to listen to Steven A. Smith's First Take sports cast highlighting a baseball player from the Yankees hiding an injury to get signed. They saw that program earlier, doing their best to distract me from sinking the eight ball—the final ball to win the game.

I sink it like I always do, then place the cue stick on the wood part of the table.

"Too easy," I say, walking to where Alex placed my beer.

"Rack 'em. I'll show you *too easy*." Duncan shouts.

"That's the last game. I have to see...," I struggle to tell them who I want to see, realizing I don't even know her name. "The new neighbor. I don't even know her name," I inform them while picking up the empty beers to take to the sink.

The lower level of my home is an oasis for the guys. I believe they all like the manly accents, and I don't bother them about the mess they make. However, Duncan dislikes using coasters, and I do not like the water ring his beer makes on the coffee table. I give him a look, and he grins, then places a coaster under his beer.

Alex assists with retrieving the bottles and accompanies me to the second kitchen, which is hidden away at the far end of the space, away from the wet bar area.

"What is the plan when you see her? I mean, you

said she was rude to you," Alex inquires.

"Hmm, I'm not sure." I think about it for a second. "Maybe ask her for her name to start."

Alex's laughter catches me off guard. "We are in private security, database protection, and..." he pauses, then looks around and waves his hand in the air. "You know nothing about a woman who lives three doors down from you," he chuckles. "This is really rich, even for you."

"Huh? What am I supposed to be do then, stalk her?" I question Alex.

Kevin struts before us as if he heard our conversation and yawns as if bored.

"No, because your cat already stalked her." He laughs at his joke, then adds. "Look in your fancy homeowner's directory or give me her name, and I'll enter it into the Gnosis software."

My eyes light up at the thought that I can find out anything about her with a tap of the keyboard.

Alex created Gnosis using proprietary software that taps into various information sites. All our clients are screened through Gnosis, which proves the software's helpfulness in identifying risks and assessing whether the client is hiding secrets.

Gnosis was helpful in the case that Smitten is leading; although the preliminary findings have already started, the meat and potatoes will start tomorrow. We studied the Danvers Research Lab's CEO background, and my interest in her almost made me relent and take the lead on her case. However, the owner has two strikes: her last name and the fact that she manages research facilities. In my opinion, it's a fancy name for a laboratory and experiments.

"Wait, her name won't be in the directory. She mentioned she moved in three months ago," I inform Alex. "Wait, I have an idea, I'll be back."

Stepping over Kevin, I ran upstairs quickly to retrieve the community's quarterly newsletter, knowing they had a section introducing new homeowners for the year.

Hurrying past Duncan, who is now sprawled out on the sofa, cue stick still in hands, his eyes half-closed, watching Sunday baseball highlights.

I take a swig of beer, and with excitement, I place the newsletter on the counter. "Her name should be in the New to the Community section." I tell Alex.

The more pages I turn, the more frustrated I get that I can't find the page faster. "It seems there is a Summer Festival next week and a Pickleball tournament." I eye Alex, who is looking at me in bewilderment.

"This is your monthly newsletter?" Alex asks, "Here, let me look; I can scan faster." He grabs the magazine that I was so happy about its volume earlier for helping me hide my cock outline in my joggers, but now has me cursing the tedious articles in the book. *The HOA here is certainly thorough.*

"I found it," Alex says, his eyes widening as he looks at me. "Duncan, get in here; you can't miss this!" He shouts.

"What?" I don't wait for him to continue before asking, "Come on, what is her name? Do we know her?" I try grabbing the newsletter magazine, but he stiff-arms me.

Duncan comes barreling in, almost stepping on Kevin. "For fucks sake, where is the fire?" He yells, on high alert.

"You are not going to believe this," Alex laughs.

"What!" Duncan and I shout in unison, causing Kevin to run into my office den, away from the commotion.

"Deidra Danvers is Gavin's *neighbor*."

Duncan blinks his eyes. "You mean the chick he is kicking us out to see at the pool?"

"Yes," Alex confirms, slamming his hand on the counter for effect while laughing uncontrollably. "The very one."

Duncan shakes his head and narrows his eyes, pausing in deep thoughts.

"The one that Smitty is afraid of and begged for Gavin to take point?" Duncan questions, his brows high.

Alex nods. Now, they are both laughing at my expense.

"You went on and on about the name Ms. Danvers from some book earlier about how the name creeps you out," Alex says between chuckles. "Your *woman's* name is

Danvers."

"She is not my woman," I reply. *At least not yet.*

"I want to know how a name in a book can get under your skin so much that you won't take the lead on a case," Alex asks with his hand firmly on Duncan's shoulders as if to hold him up because the laughing is about to make him fall.

"You guys know my mother was an English teacher, and I love reading," I say, feeling the need to explain myself. "I read the book *Rebecca* as a kid. In it, the housekeeper was a scary figure who terrorized a poor newlywed woman everywhere." Alex and Duncan keep laughing. "Seriously, I used to have nightmares about Ms. Danvers."

Alex exhales a long sigh. "Well, the name fits this person. Smitty is terrified of her." Alex continues, "But you don't want to switch." He grows quiet, obviously understanding my plight, but he continues gingerly. "Even though we told you it's a research facility, you went on," he hits Duncan on the forearms and then points to me like I don't remember what I said. "You went on to say protecting scientists is a perfect job for Smitty; you can manage with backup away from the facility, but not point."

"But Smitty *did* say she was hot," Duncan butts in, hesitation etches on his face. "I mean professionally." He turns to Alex. "If this is a new job, I can switch the Connely engagement with Smitty. It's a walk in the park, anyway, ending soon."

"Alex can't authorize that." My voice is territorial. I

grit my teeth and continue. "From going over the files, her scientists are receiving death threats."

Before we started grilling, we went over the contract and the case. I was intrigued by the young woman's story. Last week, I instructed the team to install various jamming devices at the scientist's homes because I sensed they were being stalked. We wondered why Ms. Danvers was not receiving threats if her employees were.

Walking to my office, I took the iPad and reviewed the files we discussed earlier, ensuring we took all the necessary steps to help her company.

"We have our team with the remaining scientists in safe houses. She initially had six in the D.C. lab, but two relocated to other research facilities, and two quit?" I recall what we went over earlier.

"Yeah," Alex chimes in. "And when Smitty mentioned she might be in danger, she refused to have a tail on her." Mirth fills his eyes, and he smiles wickedly. "You said with a name like Danvers, she might not need protection."

Duncan slaps his massive hand on his head and starts shaking it. "Talk about words coming back to bite you."

Ignoring him, I start to dial the cell phone.

"Who are you calling?" Alex asks, his voice high in curiosity.

I turn my back to Duncan and Alex, whose voices are at a fever pitch in laughter. I see Kevin dart upstairs; he must sense I am about to get angry.

"Smitty, why do you want out of the Danvers case?" I didn't exchange pleasantries.

"Hey boss, I mean I can do it...she, she is just difficult, and she makes me nervous."

"Difficult, how?"

"She just gives everyone a hard time. We met with her team last week, and the men are terrified of her."

"Well, you don't have to worry. I am taking over the crew and the case."

He stutters, "Thank you, boss. I honestly wanted Alex to ask you because you seem better suited to take the lead." He replies with trepidation in his voice.

"How so?" I ask.

"She uses big words, and she taunts us, we feel," he hesitates. "We feel like she can dissect us in the lab and feed us to the plants they grow."

The fellas start laughing vigorously.

"That is far-fetched; why would the team think that?" I ask, shushing Alex and Duncan, who are gaggling.

"She nonchalantly told the team that," his voice hitches. "When setting up cameras and going through the company's server. She didn't like it when we told her we would eventually need access to *her* emails and phone records."

Duncan and Alex's eyes widen as Smitty's voice shakes over the phone speaker. "She uses big words that Stan has to look up to decipher; I think she does it on purpose to get her way."

Alex interjects, "Gav, you can match her taunts with your love for literature and robust vocabulary. Face it, you are perfect for the point on this case."

I nod but know I am not ready to go near any research center or labs.

"Duncan, Alex, and I will review the files again," I retort. "I feel like something was missing."

I hear Alex and Duncan sighing in frustration. It is going to be a long afternoon, possibly evening.

CHAPTER 4 – DIEDRA

"Ms. Danvers, you are here so early," the facility security attendant, Bobby, says while waiting for me to nod for my biometric screening. I shake my head, then stay still while he conducts a biometric scan of the second phase upon entering the facility, the first being the key card access.

"The new security I hired officially starts today," I check my watch. "I wanted to be here before Mr. Smitten, the lead security contact. He will be here in an hour. They should be in intake." I inform Bobby with a smile.

Screening visitors takes about thirty minutes, so I have time to download it with my assistant and grab a coffee.

The truth is I wanted to be here two hours earlier, but after the pool party, Esmeralda tugged at my heartstrings when I saw her outside in front of the building. Her anxiety about what the women in the community gossip about her had the best of her. I gave her a pep talk and took her back to my house for margaritas.

After Esmeralda left, I couldn't sleep. Meeting all the new neighbors who promised to vote for me to be on the Homeowner's Association Board, I was on a high.

"So why do you want to be on the Spring Ridge Board? A young woman such as yourself must have other things to worry about than working for free for such a huge community," I recall Mr. Mullins saying after I received applause when Carol introduced me.

The real reason has nothing to do with what I said.

"I have many skillsets and can add value to this awesome and welcoming community of lovely people." The room filled with more applause.

The real reason is that the HOA's president is insisting on giving a lucrative landscaping contract to one of the most notorious chemical-wielding companies in the United States.

I wrote a study about the harmful effects of pesticides on the environment, and my company discovered a plant-based alternative to what we use to kill weeds. The Management Company disregarded my claims. I decided to run when I discovered an opening on the board of directors, as if I had nothing on my plate.

My assistant, Irene, greets me after I say goodbye to Bobby; her steps are whimsical, just like her personality.

"I bought you your favorite iced caramel coffee, but it must be watered down by now," my assistant, Irene, quips.

"I keep telling you not to buy me coffee; the one in the break room is fine," I say with a smile. "Thanks for coming in early. I wanted to get here earlier, but my alarm didn't go off." I lie to my eager assistant, whose glasses are too big for her cute face and button nose, but the bright red frames complement her smooth mahogany skin.

My delay was because of being up all night, fantasizing about Mr. Bright and how he would react if I bit his nipple and tugged at his piercing with my teeth. I shiver at the thought, causing Irene to look at me. "Everything okay?" She asks.

"Yes," I answer, reaching for the heavy glass door that opened when I scanned my thumb to the data key on the side.

This damn neighbor has me thinking about his upturned full lips when he grins, those silver eyes, and the way his butt looks when he ran up the stairs.

It's been almost five damn years since I did the nasty, and Bright's body is one that I could definitely do the nasty with.

The heavy door opens, and I turn to Irene, "Come in. I'll fill you in."

Irene started as an intern working in the labs when I hired her. Realizing that research wasn't her forte, I spontaneously hired her as my assistant when my former assistant unexpectedly eloped and quit without notice. She is more than an assistant; she is like my best friend.

"Are you sure he said coffee, tea, or the door to you?" Irene asks, covering her mouth while giggling.

"Right?" I sigh, sitting back in my chair. "He's got some nerve, and supposedly, the community thinks he is so polite and charming."

"And you weren't rude first, Deidra?" she questions, darting her eyes and wringing her hands as if she doesn't want to say something, but eventually she adds, "You know, sometimes you can be so harsh with your words. And..." She stretches the word. "When you get nervous, you state random facts that can appear callous if people don't know you."

"I guess I didn't tell you I called him a narcissist and accused him of training Trixie to get my things to bring to him." I close my eyes, waiting for her to rebuke me.

"Deidra." She rolls her eyes. "Those are important details."

Our snickers last five minutes until we catch our breaths to focus on the workload.

We discussed the planning for the week's events, including a special planning session about the Thursday meeting with the SEC and the plan the security firm implemented, in which they secured two loyal scientists to the safe house.

Recalling the events when the two holdouts stood firm in the meeting with the security makes my heart warm.

"I worked for your father's small laboratory, and I was so proud of you when you took hold and grew the company to what it is now," Dr. Robben said when he accepted the security detail. "Other research facilities wouldn't have been awarded with the pattern stakes and the profit sharing you offer employees."

"*I agree, Ms. Danvers,*" added Dr. Crammer, our leading botanist. "*I understand both sides and don't blame the others for leaving after the last event, but I feel safe, and the added protection that is provided adds more comfort.*"

Our scientists have been getting threats for the past six months. Phone calls telling them to leave Danvers Research or else. From my understanding, the word *else* means dangerous events would befall them.

Most of them ignored the emails and the threats, but after receiving the latest one, two quickly exited. The perpetrators made the most heinous threat written in animal blood on the doors of where they lived. It was written in cow's blood: *Working for Danvers will lead to your peril.*

When our in-house security and local police could not identify what was on the doors or find clues, not even a figure on a Ring camera, my younger sister, a qualified scientist in her own right, recommended that we hire an outside firm to examine the threat with fresh eyes.

The renowned team of B. D. Cortez and Associates Protection Services was hired two weeks ago and discovered in a day that the doorbell cameras around the scientist homes had been disabled with a scrambling device that emitted scanners blocking visual feeds.

"Why don't you have your own guard?" Irene stands up and puts her notebook to her side.

"*Because* I don't need one if they wanted to harm me, they had ample opportunity." I slide out of my seat to show her my bravado, but the intercom buzzes, startling me. I giggle and then relax.

"Yes?" I answer the call box, knowing automatically that Mr. Smitten and his team must be arriving. "Keep them there; they will never find my office. Irene will be coming out to escort them to the conference room," I say, permitting Bobby to let the team enter the elevator to the C suite level.

The C suite level is on the same level as Bobby; when you enter, the door opens on the other side—a careful security measure I worked out for the executives.

Irene nods her head. "I'll settle them in and alert them you'll be there in a few minutes."

"Perfect," I say as she reaches for her lab coat and pulls on the door. I add, "This will give me enough time to check in with Robben and Crammer. They are due to start work in a few weeks, at least a month when the security firm guarantees they can eliminate the threat."

"I will be glad when this whole ordeal is over with." Irene closes the door as I dial Dr. Robben.

CHAPTER 5 - DEIDRA

Walking towards the conference room, I felt a bit subconscious about my dingy lab coat, which sports what looks like a grass stain in the pocket area. The dark green contrasts the coat's white color so vividly. I decided to wear it anyway because we are taking the security team on a tour of the lab since they insisted on meeting and interviewing the lab techs.

I frown when I notice it is also wrinkled and does nothing for my appearance.

Mr. Smitten and his staff have already met with me, and some of my staff members will be working with their team. First impressions are no longer needed.

As I turn the hallway's corner, I hear a cackling laugh. I was surprised to hear Irene's hearty chatter, which is uncharacteristic of her professional demeanor. "Please call me Irene. Can I get you more coffee?" Her voice fills the hallway.

Irene despises serving guests visiting the center. I recall in the Austin office when Cambridge's ecology fellows wanted to observe our cutting-edge research on the effects of germinating weeds to fight other weeds for the day. Irene was adamant about not serving them. She even brought the blonde administrative intern to help set up the coffee and snack station.

"I don't know what they think this is; my Black self is not serving any of these uppity clowns." I chuckle, remembering the events that day and admiring her conviction. But who is this girl giggling? It sounds like she is using her flirting voice.

I open the door just a bit, peeping in to see what is happening. My gaze meets Irene, who is standing at the front of the conference room table. Her smile is radiant and uplifting when she spots me. I smile back, raising an eyebrow at her while motioning with my hand for her to come closer to the door so I can ask what is going on.

She waves at someone, most likely the guy at the end of the table, and comes to me as I whisper, "Did your body get snatched by aliens? You are asking men, the patriarchy, that you, *Irene Cummings*, despise serving, is shucking and jiving to serve them," I tease.

She arches her brow, ignores my attempt to check if she is all right, and waives me in. "Gentlemen, Ms. Danvers is here. Ms. Danvers, the security firm, has made a staff change. Mr. Gavin Bright will be the lead for the B. D. Cortez team."

Did she say, Mr. Bright, the same Mr. Nipple Ring Bright? I thought.

My eyes wander, peering to the other end of the long mahogany table. Gavin Bright's grey-silver eyes meet my gaze, and he perks up to give me a wink. I instinctively slip out of the drab lab coat and fold it in my lap as I take my seat facing Mr. Bright.

Looking at Irene, I widen my eyes in disbelief. She smiles back and hands me a cup of black coffee. Then, she sits in the adjacent seat to my left to take notes.

Clearing my throat and kicking my dingy lab coat under the table, I speak. "Thanks for joining us this morning. I spent a lot of time with Mr. Smitten, and I would appreciate it if someone could tell me why he is not handling our account."

Irene's head goes down as the energy in the room shifts. Three of the gentlemen seem familiar since they were with me and other team members as they discussed our firewalls, protocols, and possible data breaches last week and during the initial meetings.

Today, they were supposed to tour the lab; two will work alongside our researchers, and the others will work with our small satellite HR and accounting staff. The rest will tour the perimeter. A small van is parked on the street, observing calls in and out of the building while the offsite security staff reviews the camera feed in the building.

Why didn't anyone inform me? No respect, I thought. *Just like that, I am dismissed again.*

"Are you familiar with Mr. Smitten's plan, which was painfully arranged for the company?" I say, staring down the silver-eyed narcissist. *The gorgeous, sexy narcissist.*

He leans in, his stare matching mine. "You mean the plan he worked out and then had to change and rework because you refused to have a security detail?" A smug smile lines his face.

I notice Irene's smirk. *Whose side is she on?* One of his guys shifts in his seat. I believe his name is Sam or Stan. If he remembers my ugly exchange with the other point man, Mr. Smitten, he is familiar with my tactics.

My gaze went to another guy who was here last week; he clutched a pen and held on to the table as if he were going to be on a roller coaster ride.

My family and friends know who I am. I am stealthy. In this industry, we have cutthroats and thieves who covet ideas and formulas they themselves cannot procure.

It takes talent to do what I must do to succeed on a battlefield that is not fair. All I have is my knowledge, will, and wits. My tongue is skillful in winning any game. I am a master, a mechanic, a puppeteer who can make the most ardent opponent quiver in the corner.

"No, the plan *I* modified to allow him to understand that I am the one fucking the cat and the B. D. Cortez's team is holding the tail."

Irene winces and looks over at me. It was a calculated choice of words, but these former military special forces guys are no virgins to crude language.

I continue my assault of words. "We have a lot to lose, and I take our employee's safety seriously, but I was not a part of these *pusillanimous* threats, so I didn't feel the need to succumb to security that will do nothing but make me seem weak to my employees, and the public. I am not afraid."

Those silver eyes didn't shift or waver from my

gaze. His impressive two new team members only shifted a bit in their seats, and the three present last week looked like they were bracing themselves for an attack.

"Are you sure about that?" the sexy protector asks, leaning back in the seat. "Are you sure the threats are *pusillanimous?* I was taught to believe that all threats against women are cowardly," he intelligently argues.

Hmm, he is smart with words; I didn't say they were threatening me.

"I *was taught* that the client should be respected and informed when there is a change," I argue back. "Besides, I am not being personally threatened."

He doesn't acknowledge my declaration.

"Why did you move to a gated community with top-level security three months ago? If you don't feel *threatened?*"

His words catch me off guard, and I am about to replay them, but he adds, "Before that, you applied for and received your concealed carry permit for the 45 Glock handgun in your locker as we speak," he utters.

Leaning forward, eyeing me as he intertwines his fingers and places them on the table. *He is commanding the room. I can't let him take control.*

"You also train in mixed martial arts daily. I believe you started taking classes six months ago."

The room mumbles with oohs as the security team becomes emboldened with the swagger and awe of their new leader.

Irene's eyes are wide as saucers as she looks at me and then back to the notes she is obviously pretending to take. Her head and hands are low, and her left-hand shields the room from the pantomime she makes as her lips motion the word 'Don't.'

Easing Irene's nerves, I take control of the situation. I give him a lovely smile while reaching to remove a lint on my smooth silk gray blouse—the same color as his devilish wolf eyes. Unbothered, I take my time.

"Mr. Bright, just because you make a statement does not mean it is factual." I pause as the room inhales simultaneously as if they are in shock. I wait for the stirring to settle down.

"Relax, gentlemen, I didn't call him a liar," I sigh, but only to emphasize my pretend boredom. "You want me to admit that I am afraid. You damn right I am. I am afraid that while you make inferences that *because* I received my concealed carry permit, *I am afraid*. However, I apply for permits in every new state that does not have reciprocity with my existing gun permits."

I walk over to the coffee station, grab the cream, and walk back. It's all done for dramatic flair.

"I am new to Virginia, so I applied for a license to carry. I am a marksman and like practicing on the gun range."

Sam or Stan looks at his colleagues, no doubt prepping them for what will come next. I continue with my rant as I take my seat and pause.

"I started training in mixed martial arts at the mere age of twelve; I am a black belt in Jin Jitsu. My practice has lapsed because," I shrug, and I look around, trying to meet their gazes, but they all look in Mr. Bright's direction, except Mr. Bright's eyes transfix on me as I continue. "Because I am busy trying to take this company public. We live in the same gated community," I arch my left brow. "Please tell me, Mr. Bright, what are *you* are afraid of."

There was another gasp, and it didn't come from Irene. I believe it came from the sandy-blonde gentleman who gripped his pen so hard that I could see the blood draining from his index finger and thumb.

The Wolf clears his throat. The only sound in the room was the slight buzzing of the machinery of the air conditioning unit.

"I am afraid that the community will never be the same with a person like you coming into my neighborhood," Mr. Bright answers.

The room blurts out in laughter as he smirks. He looks at the team and then at me. A pensive look meets his face when he peers at me, sort of an unrequited apology as if he knows he went too far.

He did go too far.

"Irene, please alert the staff that we have a delay and take Mr. Bright's team to the cafeteria," I say, trying to address the team, which had a few nervous faces but a few proud of the new lead man.

There was no movement until Mr. Bright gave

them a nod. *Impressive.* I can sense the relief in their eyes as they head toward the door.

Before they can exit, I confidently state, "Mr. Smitten will most likely replace your new lead. So, I appreciate your patience as I speak to Mr. Bright."

"It's Gavin. Please call me Gavin. Mr. Smitten has been reassigned." He rises out of his seat but doesn't turn to his team to address them. His stare never left my face. "See you soon, fellas. We'll straighten out this misunderstanding," he states calmly to the men as my stomach tightens at his direct command.

The men bob their heads in agreement and, from the looks of them, can't get to the door exiting the room fast enough.

CHAPTER 6 – DEIDRA

Picking up my cell phone, I start to dial the contact Mr. Smitten gave me on Friday.

My fingers couldn't dial fast enough. *How dare he?* He brought up my personal information to make me look bad in front of my team—oh well, *his* team. I look down at the table, but he is gone. *What the...*

"Aren't we going to talk?" he says, staring down at me.

Good gosh. How does one move so fast? Forget calling him a wolf – What is he a vampire?

"I'm calling your boss." I huff and continue. "You've disrespected me in front of the team hired to protect my employees."

He pulls out the chair where Irene sat earlier and plops his big body down, never taking his eyes off me. He squints when I speak to Mr. Cortez's manager, but he keeps smiling when I tell her that the new guy, they replaced Smitten with is not a good fit and that I want him to be reassigned.

When I hung up the phone, he let out a sigh. "Are you done?"

"No, you are the one who is done," I answer, folding my arms across my chest and tapping my feet. My body is riddled with energy. "Your office will call you shortly to replace you and put Mr. Smitten back on our case."

His cell phone rings. I can't help but uncross my arms and pull up a seat next to him, giving him an "I told you so" look.

"That is probably them now," I exclaim smugly.

"Hmm." He looks at his phone. "You are right; that is *them*."

I almost feel bad for him, but who is he to look up my background? *I wonder how much he knows about me anyway.* My eyes go wide when I notice him putting his phone on speaker so I can hear.

"I am sorry to disturb you, sir," says a voice like Jarvis, Iron Man's assistant; my nephew Ben loves Iron Man, and I watched a marathon with him last time I was home. Jarvis continues, "I know you changed the schedule and took the lead on the Danvers case, but Ms. Danvers demands that Mr. Smitten return. We all know he doesn't want to do it. The men are saying she is a beast, sir."

He smirks coyly. "Did you explain to her that Mr. Smitten is not available and that the CEO and founder of the company will be handling her case personally?"

"We tried to, sir, but she wouldn't let us get a word in." He pauses, and I hear the tension in his voice. "Perhaps we can ask Alexander Donnely to assist?"

"Nah, I'll let her know, and thanks for taking this

on, Gregory," he says with a cocky smile on his face.

"Thank you so much, sir. Have a great rest of your day." The uptight Jarvis hangs up.

The cocky smile grows wider.

"That was not the person I spoke with. I spoke to Alexander Donnely's admin." I say, standing up to my full height.

He reaches for my hands. I back away from him, which causes him to chuckle this time.

"Gregory Adams is *my* executive assistant. The young woman you spoke with is Tami, my business partner's executive assistant." He steps closer. "I know it must be confusing."

"Confusing, I am not confused, and I want you gone like bubbles."

He laughs. "You want me gone like bubbles, meaning, gone in a flash because bubbles don't stay around long?"

"I'm surprised you got that," I slip the quick insult in. "Tell me why you think I am confused about Alexander Donnely's admin. He signed the contract, did he not?"

His eyes narrow as he answers, "I am the founder and CEO of B.D. Cortez and Associates, you heard Smitten is unavailable. Frankly, he doesn't want to work for you. His words, not mine." He begins quoting with quotes. "She is demanding, arrogant, and a know-it-all," he huffs, not seeming to mince words. "My business partners are

Alexander Donnely and other Marines from my Recon squad. We would love to follow the plan that *we* worked out together."

The arrogant prick stares at me, his silver-gray eyes shining in the office's white light. Although the light is supposed to be unflattering, those eyes captivate me and beckons me to do naughty things to him.

He thinks he has bested me. He holds my cat hostage and calls him Kevin; he dismisses me, and it seems my presence bothers him. He owns the company I rely on to protect us, yet he wants to show me up at every encounter.

I am who I am because I don't give up, and I don't let anyone control my fate.

In the words of William Ernest Henley from Invictus, I am the captain of my ship, so as I get up and head for the conference room door, I utter three words to him. "You are fired." But he doesn't want to listen. He grabs my forearm and pulls me back, back into him, causing me to bump into his hard body. He backs away awkwardly.

Why does he feel so good? I eye his big hand on my forearms. I see the veins pulse through the back of his hand. *Oh Lord, what is this man doing to me?*

"You want to win so badly that you will endanger your team." His silver eyes stare down at me. "Our Gnosis platform says that whoever is doing this has just started. They started with the low-hanging fruit. You have 45 labs and research facilities. Your headquarters are in Austin, where your sister lives, yet there have been no threats.

You came to this facility eight months ago; the threats were present but not seen."

Get it together, Deidra; how can one man have this effect on you?

"What the heck is a Gnosis?" I ask, trying not to look at those full lips. *Why does he have such full, juicy lips?* My nether region is stirring, causing me to clench my thighs together for relief.

He frowns as he looks down at his hand still on my left forearm.

"On Sunday evening, we disabled a device that scans data from your email and all your employer's email," he says as he rubs my arm. "The threat is real, and they want you."

My sister is right. I am such a brat. I knew all along that whoever or whatever this threat was, it was after me. They want to take me down. They want to see me weak and all I have done to be successful, fail.

I planned to get this center up and running. I only need one year, one freaking year, and Danvers will be a public lab competing with the big boys. However, I exceeded expectations, and I am meeting with the SEC officials on Thursday to hopefully achieve our goals.

Looking up at him with his rugged features. He looks like he could be the owner of the research center. The rich smell of his earthy cologne, the crisp white shirt, and the dark blue suit tailored over his bulging muscles cover his beautiful artwork. He smiles contritely, and I feel like I am floating.

I slap his hand off my forearm to free myself. He doesn't waiver. He is still in my space, his gray-silver eyes glaring.

I am stealthy, I am bold, and I am a force.

I pretend to whisper for him to lean in. He looks puzzled and leans in to hear what I have to say, but I don't want to say anything to him. I *need* to do something *to* him…

I am bold, stealthy, and I am also horny.

It's been five whole years since I have touched a man, kissed a man, or held a man.

I grab the back of his neck and guide his face down to meet mine. I stretch and stand on my tippy toes to press my lips upon his and suck those beautiful full lips.

Damn, they feel oh so good, soft yet firm. I suck and kiss, waiting for him to allow my tongue to enter. I dare him to refuse what his body language has been relentlessly trying to convey, practically screaming to me yesterday and across the conference table.

I dare him to deny me and to deny this kiss.

CHAPTER 7 – GAVIN

What the fuck, she is in the dominant role? I pull her close to me, her body soft and inviting. Her tongue wants to enter, and I open for her, oh how I open for her.

She read my mind. All I wanted yesterday and today was her. I wanted to kiss her, but she is technically my boss; *we work for her*, the impropriety, the unprofessionalism of it all. The way her body feels against mine. I must assert my masculinity, take control, and deepen the kiss.

I have never been kissed like this, kissed like we are on fire in an arid forest, dry and hoping for rain. That hope flees when impulses disregard all consequences and light a small match, lending way to a raging wildfire consuming everything in its path. I am not thinking about repercussions; *I want her.*

She intimidates the most hardened Marine. I noticed that the men who were here last week wouldn't meet her gaze or look in her direction. Stan tells me that it was so confusing to look at her: "It was like she looked like a Disney princess, but when she spoke, she was the villain."

Our verbal sparring in front of my staff triggered my cock, making it so hard it strained against my pants. My mind groped for words. Just touching her forearm and holding her arm in my hand felt like I crossed a line. We are now crossing the equator, the longest line ever crossed.

Her fingers caress the back of my neck, her tongue darts in and out of my mouth, and she wrestles mine for dominance, but I must teach her a lesson. I will start by educating her that she is not in control, nor am I in control, but the need between has become untenable to control. It must be quenched.

We both pause as if we are choreographing this wanton display, but my flesh needs to be inside her. I lose control, lifting her while looking into her sweet brown eyes.

The conference room's warm white light cast shadows of her long lashes fanned on her cheeks. Her breaths are music playing in this mesmerizing dream concert where desire takes center stage. I place her on the conference table. Not taking my eyes off her, I carefully unbutton her silk blouse.

I am in a haze as I stare at her round, full breast encased in a delicate red lace bra, her nipples poking out taut and rigid. Brushing my thumb over one nipple, I see her collapse and hold on to the conference table. With no hesitation, I suck those buds pushing the lace to the bottom. *I can't stop.*

The impropriety of my actions is in the back of my head. Now I understand why those sailors could not resist the sirens calling them to their deaths in Greek mythology. *She is going to lead to my disaster—a disaster so sweet that it will end me.*

My cell rings, a mere annoyance but not enough to break my trance. I look down at her perfect mounds, wet from my deeds, and the inconvenience of the red lace bra will soon be removed.

My cell rings again. My predator is also in a trance, sitting on the conference table with her eyes closed like those sirens. My cell rings again. This time, I back away and turn to answer it.

"Get a hold of yourself, man." Alex's voice on the other end wakes me from the daze.

CHAPTER 8 – GAVIN

"Huh?" is all I can say. "I mean, Alex, what you got." I think I have recovered nicely.

"What protocols do we take for our clients when there is a threat to life?"

"Now is not the time," I whisper. "I am in the middle of something," I grunt out.

"Damn right, you *were* in the middle of something." His voice is irritatingly louder. He repeats, speaking through clinch teeth. "What are the protocols, Gav? Name the steps, the ones we don't *share* with the client."

My eyes blink rapidly. *Fuck.* I turn around to see Danvers, my siren, hopping off the conference table and buttoning up her blouse as if knowing that the moment has ended. She closes her eyes and blows a deep sigh while her head shakes back and forth in regret.

"What are the protocols? Why did Smitten's team need access to all the conference rooms?" Alex continues to harass me.

I run my fingers through my hair as if my fingers could be the conduit to put sense in my brain. Of course, the first protocol was to place spy cameras in the common rooms, the kitchen, conference rooms, and the rooms where in-house security doesn't check. The revelation crept up, hitting hard my serious infraction of the rules.

"I know, I know," I say, not saying aloud that the protocol is to *surveil the area* without notifying the client. *Is my team watching me put the client in a compromising position?*

Alex continues as if he heard my thoughts. "They contacted me. I told them to shut down the cameras for now." Alex's voice sounds more disappointed than upset. "You have worked hard to get here, man. What are you doing? Get a grip."

I didn't wait for him to hang up. Deflated, I hang up.

"Ms. Danvers?" I clear my throat and turn to the client, who must be referred to as the client. "I am not sure what just happened, but it can never happen again. If you want Mr. Smitten," I don't meet her eyes when I exhale, "we can bring him back."

She looks at me and then down at her silver silk blouse, guiding me to follow her gaze. I look to where her eyes went; her shiny silver silk blouse has two wet spots courtesy of my overzealous sucking and kissing. It would be funny if the situation were not so dreadfully embarrassing.

"First off, you can call me Deidra. I think we earn the right to be on a first-name basis," she answers. "And I would have stopped it before we got too far."

"Here take my jacket." I hand her my jacket, but she slaps my hand away.

"Are you crazy?" She hisses. Her eyes dart back and forth. "Do you want your team to speculate *why* I needed your jacket?" She starts fixing her hair and kneels to the ground. My cock instantly gets hard with anticipation. However, she goes under the table to retrieve a dingy lab coat. "See, that's better," she says while putting it on.

She whispers, clenching her teeth. "And I hear the elevator. The team is back." She hurries down the hall and shakes her head when I try to follow her. "There's no need to follow me, and I don't want Smitten. You are the right man for the job. Irene will show you around. I forgot I have an appointment. I will circle back later to ensure everyone is situated."

She looks like a speed walker, shifting from foot to foot as she disappears from my sight.

"Everything okay, boss?" Stan, a staple on Smitten's team, asks as he approaches me from the elevator. "Are you leaving us?"

I turn around and shake my head more to shake off the haze of what just occurred.

"No, I am going to be on point," I turn to look at the team. "Let's get these bastards."

If I were to pinpoint a specific time when morale changed at a specific job, this would be one of those moments. Cheerful and optimistic faces met my gaze, and one of the cheeriest of them was Irene, a Danvers employee looking down at her phone and carefully examining a message she had received.

"Unfortunately, Ms. Danvers was called away to

handle an important matter. After the tour, she will join us later in the downstairs conference room," Irene, the loyal assistant, says while pressing the down button for the elevator.

Whispers and mumbles filled the hall. I know why Ms. Danvers won't participate in the tour, but I must play my part. "Right, we agreed that Ms. Cummings knows this facility inside and out. She is an outstanding replacement," I affirm.

"Awe, thanks, Mr. Bright." Irene gives me a cheerful look, "The first stop is the lab. We have to take important steps to ensure everyone's safety. Please follow me."

The elevator opens, and we all pile in to go to the other elevator. She presses the first-floor button, which reads "Research Lab" in small letters.

If I could see Deidra again, I would be willing to tolerate the lab and data center tours. However, this is the equivalent of having no reward, only punishment. The sweat on my forehead begins to form.

"The Danvers Research Lab Facility is a busy laboratory with protocols prioritizing safety and confidentiality. The research and data center tour ends here, now for the lab." Irene walks briskly to the end of the bustling data center to a double glass door flanked by security checkers and biometric readers.

"Upon entering the lab, you will notice multiple security measures in place. Access to the lab is restricted to authorized personnel only, with keycard entry systems and biometric authentication. This ensures that only approved individuals can enter and work within the premises."

Irene looks behind her, ensuring that the team follows her. Stan hung on to her every word, but for me, it was the opposite. The more she talks about the lab protocols, the more my hearing becomes fainter, with my palms clammy.

"What is it, Mr. Bright?" Irene's face looks puzzled as she eyes my raised hand.

"The team received clearance, but..." I say, clearing my throat. I look beyond the glass doors and observe individuals dressed in lab coats similar to the ones we were given. Individuals wearing safety goggles and gloves. The bright lights made the scene more hard-core because they highlighted every sample of test samples and fluids the researchers were observing.

Even though the scientists work diligently in their stations, the structure seems chaotic.

"I don't need to see the lab. " I say, pointing to the chair near the security checkpoint. "I will just wait here." One of the attendants looks at us in confusion.

My team gives me an awkward smile. "We have the blueprints showing the lab layout, and the emergency exit is secured to ensure no one can enter, exit only," Stan says, tucking proudly on his lab coat.

As the team entered the lab, relief went through my body. I inhale, taking a deep breath, which gives some support as slow breaths come as I count in my head.

I know specimens are kept in a contained environment, and the area is safe, but my mind is unprepared for the encounter. As I count my last set of numbers to match my breath, I think about Deidra Danvers.

Duncan, Alex, and I intensely studied Danvers' background. Born to the mistress of Frank Mitchell, her father. Deidra came to live with the family after her mother committed suicide when she was nine years old, but it took a year before Mr. Mitchell brought her to the house. His wife, who was battling cancer, died before she was allowed to live with the family.

There was a hostile takeover of the failing family business ten years ago, in which Deidra muscled her way to earn most of the shares. She did not disclose to the employees that she was in charge until two years after the takeover, when the company turned a profit. She has spent the last seven years in control of the company but hides the revelation that she is responsible for exponentially growing the network and net worth. They are on track to become the first Black-owned research facility to go public.

I was amused to discover that every time she set up another research facility, she bought a home and rented it out to single mothers at a discounted rate. She undoubtedly appreciates the meager upbringing she experienced while living with her mother.

My cell rings once again today, releasing me from my thoughts.

"So, you couldn't go into the lab?" Alex's voice seems concerned through the other end of the phone. "Listen, man, we know what you had to go through *there*.

Don't let it interfere with the job." There is a pause. I know he is waiting to assess my response, but I have none to give him. He continues chastising me. "Smitten could go through the lab, and he is far from attracted to the client."

"Stop, just stop, Alex." I adjust my earpiece so he can hear my resolve. "I am the right guy to work point on this assignment. Don't make me pull rank on you." I remind myself that two guards stood within four feet of hearing my conversation. I start walking away toward the data center to deliver my argument, but he interrupts.

"Gav, I can't imagine what you went through at the hands of those animals, and I believe you when you said you received," his voice trails off as if he is going to say a dirty word, and he does say it, "*therapy*, but you are not a machine. What they did to you, your body..."

I cut him off before he could finish. "God damn it, Alex, that was years ago, a decade. And it was nothing compared to what they did to Cortez." I grit my teeth. The pressure in my head is at a fever pitch, causing me to walk back to the attendant guys to take a seat. "Trust me, I got this. Smitten is good, but I am better suited. We are not going to talk about it again. Agreed?"

"What about Diedre Danvers?" he questions.

"What about her?" I counter.

"What happened earlier must not happen again, Gav, you know. What were you thinking?"

"The thing is, I wasn't thinking. Yeah, it won't happen again." I look down at my cock. It got instantly hard when my mind went back to the encounter, as it was to say, '*Not if I had anything to do with it.*' It gives me comfort to know that as fucked up as my mind is sometimes, my body is on autopilot and wants what it wants.

"Smitten has set up a Zoom with Frank Mitchell to discuss his statements about the competitors his daughter had buried over the last seven years. Would you like to debrief with Smitten?"

"I got all I need from him. Talk later." I say, quickly ending the call. Annoyance curses through me at the thought of how he painted Deidra to be demanding and aggressive and what he wrote in the files. A word often used as code to target people of color. Deidra Danvers challenging? Yes, Bold? Definitely. Assertive? Oh yes. However, the words he used in the files were words that were not suitable for any client. Difficult and aggressive.

"That term is used to paint people like me to give others the excuse to see me as less than," Cortez says as we huddled together cold in the enemy's truck bound, riding for what seemed like days. "My mom is the bank manager back home, and sure enough, every time she was to get a raise, they would call her in to say that she doesn't smile enough or she is too 'aggressive' with the other managers."

"That sucks." I adjusted myself to lay my back against the moving van's wall. My gaze met Cortez. "But we have more important issues," I said with a little chuckle but winced in pain, which is an indication of a cracked rib, maybe more than one.

Cortez looked up at me with a pained expression. He was still pinned on his side hog-tied because he was deemed aggressive. I did most of the fighting.

"I see your point," I said, remembering that the Chechen rebels spoke Russian, which I am fluent in. "This one here is very aggressive."

"Sir, sir. Ms. Cummings has been calling you. Are you okay? Stan's hands were on my shoulder, shaking me from my deep, disturbing memories.

I look up to see my team and Irene Cummings staring at me as if they are all observing a specimen that just got pulled into their dimension.

"Pardon me," I say. "I was deep in thought, reviewing some items in the case." Thinking I was recovering, I stood up. "That was a swift tour." I chuff to change the mood.

"Where is Deidra?" Ms. Cummings asks, stepping towards me. "She texted me that she was on her way here to take you to the conference room on this floor to review employee's schedules after you told me you didn't want to do the tour."

I look at my watch.

"That was almost fifty minutes ago? Call her." I demand.

"I just did, and it went straight to voicemail."

"Stan, call the tech support, tell them to give us the feeds out of the executive offices, scrub from forty-five minutes to now."

"No need. I can pull them up on my screen." In a swift movement, Stan takes out a small device and punches in some buttons quickly.

My heart went cold when we saw the scrambling signal, similar to the one when the blood spilled at the entrance of the scientist's doors.

I dash to the elevator, taking off the far too-small lab coat. My team follows suit, guns drawn.

Shouting back to Stan. "Stay with Ms. Cummings and the attendants and give the signal to lock down the facility. No one goes in or out."

CHAPTER 9 – DEIDRA

(One hour earlier)

"That is the thing, Sis. I wasn't thinking; I was doing. Just don't say I told you so," I say into my cell, my head hung down like I had committed a crime.

My younger sister, younger by three years, does just what I asked her not to.

"I told you." I can imagine the smirk on her beautiful copper-brown skin. "Your hormones are out of whack. You neglect your needs for the company." She giggles. "Five years without dick can make even the mellowest of humankind go nuts."

"What about nuns? How do they survive?" I retort.

"Don't you remember the scowls they all had at school? You know they weren't happy, walking around hitting us if we spoke out of turn or messed up the requirements to be good catholic girls."

"I remember." I nod my head even though she can't see me. "But, Bernie, I practically attacked him. What's wrong with me? I sigh, rifling in my locker to find a black T-shirt. I often wear workout clothes in case I want to get a run or a bike ride before or after work. Feeling proud of my discovery, I take my phone and go to the adjoining personal bathroom to change into the T-shirt.

"For starters, go to a bar to pick up a one-night stand, get laid. I understand that you don't want to put your profile on dating sites, but you need to get nailed and quickly before you start sexually harassing the employees or the fine silver fox in Product Development," she teases.

My mind goes straight to Derrick Johnson, the Black Brad Pitt and owner of a small sports medicine company that we recruited years ago to launch our product development team, and I swoon a bit, but my mind goes back to Gavin Bright.

"I practically sexually harassed the owner of the company that I hired to protect us from these threats."

"If you like this guy, then why don't you just ask him out after everything is over?"

"You think? Don't you think that's too bold?" I ask.

"Come on, Deidra. Bold is practically your middle name." Her tone changes. "Ben just walked in."

"You tell my nephew that I will see him soon and that I love him," I say, admiring how the black tee blends with my black skirt, almost like a little black dress. "Thanks for cheering me up, Sis. Take care."

"Deidra, *you* take care and listen to them. You can't do this alone. Think about coming home. Deidra, just come home," she says, her voice husky and broken in concern.

My sister tugs at my heartstrings. "Coming home

is not an option. I will listen. Bye for now," I respond, pushing the button on my cell to end the call. She was getting emotional, and this was no time for hysterics.

Even though I wanted to avoid feelings, my thoughts took me back to the first time I met my sister. I was a mere ten years old, and she hid behind a column at the Mitchell estate in Colorado, but she won me over when I saw her floppy bunny pink slippers sticking out, contrasting the tacky, vast obsidian columns. Although she was only seven years old at the time, I felt a sense of relief and instant love for a sister I didn't know but who was now my family. I didn't have to be alone anymore.

Can this day get any more unpredictable? I thrive on predictability, and the fact that I time block my day to the letter disturbs me. I tried to jump on the next-door neighbor like a teenager with raging hormones. Now, my sister is getting all emotional and shit worrying about me like I can't take care of myself. *I am the older sister; I can take care of myself.*

Bernadette was the apple of my father's eye, a brilliant prodigy scientist until she got pregnant with Benjamin, my nephew, ten years ago. To save the proverbial face, the family made up some story about a marriage and divorce from a well-off family that never really existed.

At first, Bernie refuses to tell us who Ben's father is, I thought it was some great clandestine affair, but one night when we got shit-faced drunk, she admitted she didn't know herself. I kept her secret. There is no judgment here. I love and respect my sister and Ben; he is also like my son. There isn't anything I wouldn't do for my nephew.

I am not even sure if Mr. Bright Eyes is attracted to me. I am disgusted with myself. Everything I take is by force, including my father's company and a meeting with the SEC representatives. One might call it blackmail, but I might have mentioned to a publicly traded competitor that I wouldn't enter the same field testing biodomes if they introduced us to the SEC auditors.

Why did I make the first move and was grinding on him like a wanton hussy? I couldn't even face him after the aftermath of the sucking of my nipples through my red lace bra. Heat rises to my face when I remember his lips.

The only serious relationship I ever had was with an egomaniac scientist, Alan Holms. A wealthy trust fund baby whom I met in grad school and when I told him about my dreams of opening a research center, he said I could work for his family, and the research center that his family owns would be the number one facility in the world. I don't know why I even accepted his proposal, but we were engaged for only two weeks. It took me *that* long to discover he was all bark, no bite. Besides, he reminded me of Frank, my father, a self-absorb ass.

I honestly don't think Alan's company will ever be the number one research facility because the last time I looked up his family's company, we were way ahead of them in botany and molecular plant research.

When I peer at the company's silver and green logo, I feel proud. My mother's name is over the area I designed for our executives, a feat that was recently completed. The spacious layout of the offices, coupled with high-quality furnishings and modern decor, creates a sophisticated space and professional atmosphere.

Irene and I carefully selected subtle designs, from the frosted patterns on the glass doors for privacy to the tasteful artwork on the wall. Once we receive approval to become a public company, we will move the executives from the Austin headquarters to D.C.

My office is in the back and requires a biometric fingerprint to open the door. Irene's office is right outside mine.

Although I visit the lab at night to review data, I rarely visit the C suites unless Irene is here. The emptiness and isolation of the space give me the creeps at night, so I also utilize a small office off the data center area.

Passing the lounge area, I again marvel at the plants and the carefully chosen color palate that contributes to the sense of refinement and luxury. The only downside to the space is the lack of people. Sighing, I think about how long it will take to transfer the executives to the C suites we've created for them. All our plans rely on if we go public.

Even the ornery old man, my father, opposed me as, in his words, pipe dreams until the acquisitions of other labs proved profitable and the growth, expansions, and revenue increased.

My cell phone rings with Irene's call, waking me from my daydream.

"Hi, Ms. Danvers; since Mr. Bright didn't enter the lab, would you like to meet him in the conference room to review personnel files like they wanted?"

"Okay," I chuckle. "I will be down in a second. See you soon," I tap the elevator button but forget my lab coat.

I return to my office to retrieve the coat; I open the door to my office and head toward the elevator again.

Changing the company's name was harder than taking it over. I know I had to play cutthroat and hide my intentions from my father, but in his eyes, I wasn't the heir apparent; it was Bernie until she got pregnant. Then, it was a distant cousin until he left Oxford. My dad planned to wait, but I eminent domain my position. I took over, tripled revenue, and doubled our research facilities.

My Dad would have chosen anyone other than the girl who was a mistake. However, I created my own destiny. I walk out to the security level, frowning as I push the button to the lower level.

In the shadows, I spot a blurry figure rushing toward me. As I turned to engage, I managed to get a hit that leveled the individual to the ground. *My training is paying off.* My ego has the best of me as I hover over his body, adrenaline-filled rage.

"You dare to come into my space and threaten my people." I kick him. Panic takes hold of me as I think about Bobby, the attendant guarding the floors to the C suite.

Where is Bobby?

I pick up my cell phone to dial 911 when another figure slams into me, causing me to topple to the ground.

Stupid, I try to engage, but he lands a hard punch to my left eye, forcing me to the ground. This guy is a lot bigger than the other one, and he sits on me, my arms pinned at my side.

Unable to strike him, I must defend myself by turning my head and making noise. Any noise, even a scream.

My scream is not coming out. It seems like my voice has left the building.

His body is heavy as he straddles me. *He owns me; he can do anything he wants.*

I am bold. I am stealthy. I ain't shit.

I think about how the executive suites failed because someone managed to bypass our security. I think of Gavin Bright and how I wish he were here, and I wonder if he will take good care of Trixie for me. The unfinished business with my father and the fuckers at the SEC that should have met last week instead of this week.

Fuck B. D. Cortez protectors because I am meeting my demise right now as this motherfucker is touching me, strangling me. I am losing consciousness. I think of ways to help myself, and when an idea reaches me, he puts one of his massive hands on my breast.

"You're not so uppity now?" the big oaf mumbles as he grinds into me.

Bile rises to my throat with disgust close behind.

Uppity? I don't even know you. You are wearing a ski mask. Is he going to...oh my god, rape me in my own building?

My voice decided it had enough of a respite. It

returned only to put me in more peril. The two words are wrapped in impetus, shouts once the elevator opens.

"Fuck you!" I scream.

Disdain shows in his eyes as they narrow. His large hand went from groping my breast under my t-shirt to squeezing my throat.

The shock of the violence reverberates through my mind, instantly filling it with a deafening feeling of regret.

I see flashing pictures of my sister Bernie, my nephew Ben, my employees, and little big Trixie the cat. Oh God, please don't let Irene find my body. Darkness is taking over me. Gavin Bright's sly smile fades to dark.

CHAPTER 10– GAVIN

It had been only 10 minutes since we discovered Deidra had gone missing. The surveillance videos showed no one leaving the building since early this morning when the janitorial staff and data researchers left their shift.

I've instructed the backup team to circle the perimeter of the building. *She is still here in the building, but where?*

Anyone entering her office needs a biometric fingerprint, and the access data software shows no one has entered since Deidra after the meeting.

"What if she is off somewhere on her own accord?" asks Mike, one of the team's newer members. I say newer, but he has been with us for one year, six months, and two days.

Ignoring his words, I pull out my cell to tell Alex to bring in more men. The static disturbances on the surveillance feed were deliberate. This was a well-orchestrated plan.

I close my eyes and curse myself for leaving her alone when she was the target all along. Hell, she knew it, too. *Did lust jade my better senses from doing my job?*

Mike and I checked the C suites, and the rest of the team searched frantically for her in the building. Before I could dial Alex, Stan came through in my SENTRY, a communication earpiece.

"Speak," is all I say to Stan.

"So, a Robert Gill access card was used to access the C suites. No one is manning the suites' entrances," he says. "We are in the conference room near the data center. The team is feeding me all the info you requested."

"Bobby, is that what they call him, the attendant at the research entrance who checks you into the executive level?" I ask, yet my voice holds a sense of calm. "Do we know where he is yet?"

"We are still searching," he responds.

"And what about the access logs?" I ask, eager for a clue.

"No one entered the C suites today except Robert Gill, Ms. Danvers, and her assistant, Ms. Cummings. It was Bobby's access that allowed us in earlier."

"Think outside the box," I say, holstering my gun. "If any unknown individual entered the C suites yesterday, check those logs," I demand.

Turning to Mike, I say. "Go down and bring Irene Cummings to me. This is not adding up."

"Roger that." The eager young spry keeps his gun cocked and sprints to the elevator.

One thing that will make finding Ms. Danvers easier is that this research center relies heavily on card key fobs and a system called PAXS that, when you swipe a section of the center, your access, including the time, is stored in a secured database. This guy probably has someone on the outside who knows how to wipe the surveillance cameras from when they entered the building, yet the cameras to enter the center and the lab were not interfered with.

Fuck, they are inside, it's an inside job.

I buzz my earpiece to alert Stan and the team when I hear Mike screaming down the hall. "Sir, come quick. I think I found something."

"On my way." Multitasking, I alert Stan to look at all the personnel. No one is allowed to leave. Danvers must be still in the building.

As I approach Mike, who has yet to exit the elevator to bring Irene back to me, he hovers on the ground near the elevator.

"What is it?" I ask, bending down to look at what he is seeing. My eyes grow wide. "How the fuck did you spot this?"

"I missed it before due to the rush to find her." His eyes gleam with pride.

A white button stood up on the silver part of the elevator—not just any old button. It came off the absurd-looking lab coat we all wore earlier. It stood there perfectly, like it was meant to be a clue.

"Stan," I shout into the comm piece. "She is still in the building but not on this floor. Her cell phone is offline, but all traces show that it's still here. Stan, do you have anything, I am coming to you." Checking my watch, I tell the team, "It's been an hour; we need infrared scanners. Get Alex on the line. Have him on when I get there."

Upon entering the small conference room, I see Stan miraculously turn it into a war room. Earlier in the elevator, I received information that caused my stomach to churn. I must fill everyone in about what happened to Robert Gills.

The room is bustling with activity as the team is feverishly working on answers. Irene has a seat and works on a laptop, accessing data points. Stan even reaches out to Smitten to offer some incitement. I am not sure he can make it since he just flew back from Missouri.

It is pleasing to know that we have access to the data systems and camera feeds from all the access points in the building hooked up to a 55-inch monitor. One guy is flipping through access points to determine any anomalies.

"Alex, are you on?" I say as I make my way to the center of the room.

"I am here, Gavin," he answers.

"I am here, too." Smitten's high-octave voice carries across the room on the other comm. Relief makes its way to my chest. I was unhappy with how Smitten painted Deidra, but we need him now. I need anyone who can help us.

I nod to the team as I make my way to the center of the small room, at the head of the table. My frame dwarfs the chair and table I stand before.

"Here is where we are and what we know," I say, my voice giving the familiar military briefing cadence the team and I are accustomed to. "At approximately zero-nine-thirty," Seeing Irene Cummings' confusion, I repeat the time. "At 9:30 AM, Ms. Danvers told her assistant that she was on her way to meet me near the lab. Her assistant said she heard the elevator chime in the background."

I begin to pace, which is a nervous habit that helps me think.

"At 11:15 AM, forty-five minutes later, she hadn't shown; now it's almost noon." Irene's eyes widen, and she continues to peek at her computer. Tears pool in her eyes. "The last signal we had from her cell indicated she was still in the building; that was an hour ago, but the signal went dead." I took a deep breath. "The guard who guarded the C suites and whose access card was used has been found bound and unconscious in one of the rooms; he was rushed to the hospital. He is in surgery, and we await hearing from him."

Irene's tears are falling on the table. She covertly tries to wipe them. She puts on her red-frame glasses as if they could protect her from feelings.

I continue the brief. "We believe Ms. Danvers left a clue; a button, perhaps from her lab coat, was found lodged in the elevator's corner frame."

Irene stands up. "That's her. I mean, that is a clue. We have a joke." Her voice trails off as she gazes at the men staring at her. Wringing her hands, she continues. "We always joke about the quality of the buttons on the lab coats, Deidra; I mean, Ms. Danvers jokes that if you wash a lab coat once, the cheap buttons are likely to fall off in the machine. See, look at mine." Her eyes are bright with hope.

I look at her coat as she closes it to show that most buttons are missing. "But that could mean that they easily fell off?" Mike interjects.

She shakes her head and closes her eyes. "That's the joke. They only fall off in the washing machine, or if you tug at them to take them off, getting a button that does not lay flat is a sign."

"Wait one sec," Stan says, staring at his monitor. "Gavin asked me to check on the access fobs looking for abnormality, including yesterday since no one entered suspiciously today."

I went to his side; Irene also met me there. He points to his screen. This person entered the C-Suite on Sunday, yesterday at 16:30, that's 4:30 PM," he smiles at Irene, "and the last time he entered was six months ago."

"Six months ago?" Irene says. "Six months ago was about when we completed the C suites renovation."

"Did contractors have access?" I ask.

"Yes, but mostly on the weekends. I am not sure, but most of the access got canceled," she frowns.

"Can you provide a picture?" I ask Stan.

"We should have his data badge linked to the system," he answers excitedly.

He begins typing. His fingers move swiftly like the thoughts in my brain.

Alex's voice booms on the telecom, anticipating my thoughts." I just checked the surveillance. It was indeed down yesterday for fifteen minutes at 16.30 PM yesterday.

"Enough time for him to come in and hide." Smitten's voice also interrupted my requests.

"Extraction teams normally work in teams of two. The other guy knew the system and knew that she would be in to get the jump on the guard. He had to have known him."

"I agree. It must be an extraction. If they wanted to kill her, they would have done so already." I chime in.

"Oh God!" Irene screams, looking at the computer. "I know him!"

CHAPTER 11 – DEIDRA

His weight feels like he is crushing me into the mattress.

He is not moving, just still; blood pours out of him like it's spraying. I cover my face and turn my head. It is not like I didn't warn him not to remove the nail that was lodged deep into his main artery.

I push and try to move him, but he is too big. His legs are twitching. Panic must have overtaken him. He stands up and then circles the foot of the bed, reminding me of a chicken with no head. He covers his neck, but it is too late - blood oozes out over his fingers. His eyes roll up in his head, and he collapses.

I breathe out a heavy scream. My scream is deafening, but only I hear it.

"Scream as much as you want. No one will hear you. This is a soundproof room." I recall what the grungy failed rapist wannabe said earlier while pointing a gun at me.

"Get up, Deidra," I shout in the room, talking to myself. "The other guy is out there. He will come back, and he will kill you when he sees what you did to his kidnapping buddy."

Tears blur my vision as I recall my plight. "No, no, Deidra, don't you dare cry. You have been in worse predicaments. You are smart; you can figure this out."

How did they manage to make a hidden bunker in my building? This means they have been planning it for a while. Or does it mean that this bunker was created to steal our experimental breakthroughs?

I recognize the creep as one of the contractors who worked on the C Suite's transformation. Earlier, they mentioned planning to keep me here for a week. The room was built to be hidden and protected from heat sensor scanners.

After frantically trying to come up with solutions, I sit on the bloody bed, recalling earlier events.

"You need to go upstairs and finish the job with the security guard." I listen in shock to the big guy as he instructs the other guy. "He saw your face."

"I had to come back, man. My access got canceled, and I hid downstairs. To get to where you were, I had to use his card."

The third-rate kidnappers argue back and forth.

"Please, you don't have to hurt him," I interject. I have money, I can reward you. Please let me go. I didn't see your face."

They wore ski masks, and I don't know who they are.

"Please, mister, don't leave me here with him." I hug myself."

It was like I was invisible. Tears rolled down my cheek. "He wants you to leave so he can rape me," I blurt out.

"I am taking the gun," he resigns. *"Promise not to hurt her."*

"I won't," the Oaf lies with a smirk. *"Scout's honor."* He held up two fingers

As soon as the other guy pulled up the ladder. The big Oaf removed his mask. My eyes grew wide with recognition. "I ain't no Scout," he scowls.

I shiver at the violent memories. I feel sick to my stomach; the smell of blood permeates the room.

My head feels like I am holding up a grand piano as I stare at several monitors highlighting what is going on within the building.

I walk towards the screen but can only move a foot off the bed rails. *Shit, I forgot my right foot is shackled.*

On the table next to the bed, there is a magazine clip with bullets and a pack of cigarettes. I didn't expect him to honor his promise.

Come on, Deidra, no one is going to save you. If only I could reach the Oaf, I could get the key in his pocket. I stretch out my body, but my hand barely touches the hair on his head; his face is buried in the mattress. *I think I am going to vomit.*

I see Gavin Bright running down the hallway on one of the monitors. They are searching for me. Thank God they didn't call the police. If they did, the spotlight would be on the company, and I would lose my bid with the SEC to go public.

Shit, my head is pounding, the adrenaline must be

wearing off. Someone, please find me before the other guy comes back.

CHAPTER 12 – GAVIN

The men and I stare at Irene, waiting for her to tell us who the picture of the man on the badge is.

"Who is he?" I ask when Stan blows up the badge of the stocky Caucasian guy with stringy blonde hair and a ragged beard.

"He was one of the contractors that worked on the executives' suites a while back. He is a huge guy. He did much more lurking than working; we asked the supervisor to limit his time. Deidra said he was creepy and eventually fired him." She hugs herself. "He made us uncomfortable, but suppose it is not him?"

"Look here," Stan says, pointing to his computer screen. "It's him. His badge was deactivated, not deleted and archived like the rest of the contractors. Another one of his teammate's badges was deactivated as well. They tried to reactivate both yesterday but only managed to activate one."

"Could it be when we discovered the data breach and installed our firewalls, we foiled their plans?" Smitten surmises.

"We obviously didn't do such a good job, the guard..."

Irene interrupts me.

"His name is Bobby." She wrings her hands.

"Yeah, Bobby recognized him. That's why he got close. The other guy waited in the C suites all night." I grimace, knowing that he was there the same time I was there, and if not for what we did in the conference room, she would have been safe.

Alex interjects as if reading my thoughts. "If they are still in the building hiding, where are they? What is the goal? Suppose we missed something, and they took her and left the premises. Eventually, the police must be called."

"Pull up the feed of where and when the cameras went down, what time and where. If they have a camera scrambler, it can only work five meters away from the target."

I expected my request to take hours, but after an hour of drinking black coffee and checking the infrared cameras for bodies. I heard a loud voice.

"It's the basement. Their scrambling system made the surveillance go down in the C Suites, where we found the security guard, Bobby, and then the basement. They must be in the basement," one of Alex's tech guys screams.

Irene's eyes widen. "The contractors had a room down there. It is easy to miss because it is hidden behind some dry walls," she explains.

"Who is closer to the basement? Tell them to meet us there, no noise. Wait. Irene, come with me, show me.

Mike, you got my six."

We use the stairs to descend four flights after determining that the elevator chime will alert the perps to our arrival—adrenaline courses through my body, as anger trails close behind.

The team had already checked the basement and doubted anyone could be there because there were no rooms, just a dank space with boilers and HVAC systems.

Irene pointed to the door and the drywall on the ground. More men poured into the basement. One whispers. "We already checked that room."

Mike and I take turns approaching the room, guns drawn. We enter but are only met with empty paint cans, ladders, rugs, and empty cots strewn around the large space. The emptiness in my soul mirrored the room and the deflated faces of my team.

We walk back to the elevator in defeat.

Irene's face shows disappointment and worry as she presses the button for the 4th floor.

"They are hiding somewhere. We will find Ms. Danvers," I assure her.

On instinct, I hop out of the elevator before the door closes.

"I'll take the stairs," I say in just enough time to see puzzling faces. I am not sure why I stepped off, but I don't want to take the stairs. I need to think. I need quiet to think.

It's like I felt her presence. I can practically smell

her perfume. I return to the contractor's dwelling. I was certain they had taken her there.

I sat on a chair in the middle of the dusty room, reviewing events in my mind. I do not care about the mess; I do not care about the fact that I am working in a research center where there is a likelihood of accidents and scientists doing ungodly experiments. All I care about is her. Damn it, we lost her on my watch.

My chest tightens as I think about the worst. She has been missing for more than three hours. *Did they leave the building? Are we missing something?*

My thoughts trail off to the words Cortez always brings up and reverberate through my head. "You live in your head, which causes anxiety. *You are* the only one hurting *you*."

CHAPTER 13 – GAVIN

Ten years ago...

The smell of burnt flesh still lingered in the air from yesterday's treatment. I recollect that the poor soul didn't return to the cell across the hall. He must have succumbed to his injuries.

Even though the glare of the white lights shines off the room's floor-length glass windows, making the whiteness feel more sterile, the stench of death still stains the room. It is the opposite of sterile; pureness is gone.

"You don't have to do this," I plea with the woman holding the syringe. I squirm and try to back away from the needle, but it's useless. I am strapped tight. This time, they secured me with double straps, including large metal claps across my neck to hold my head in place on the cold metal table, which stood upright for easy access.

The long needle pierces my skin, and I feel the cold liquid drug flowing into my bloodstream. *It won't be long now.*

The bitch offers me a smile as she wipes the puncture with an alcoholic swab. My unexpected burst of laughter catches her off guard, causing her to back away. As she raises an eyebrow, a hint of skepticism fills her eyes, perhaps silently asking how I could find humor in what lies ahead.

I stare at the hair growing out of the mole on the side of her cheek, and she blushes. "Aren't you going to ask me why I am laughing?" I snarl.

The woman's fear is palpable as she inches away, possibly nervous about the drug's impact, aware of the possibility that I could break free and harm her, just like I did earlier today to one of the guards who brought me here without the drug that increased strength.

She looks ahead past me and averts my eyes. Maybe if they don't look at us, they can justify what they are doing to us. To look at us exposes them to the fact that we are human.

"Answer me, I am talking to you, damn it," I demand. She doesn't answer; she never answers. *They never answer.*

"I find it ironic that you use a swab to clean the jab, considering that in a few minutes, they'll be coming in to tighten these straps and remove a limb or two," I say to her matter-of-factly.

She refuses to meet my gaze, her eyes darting away as I growl in her direction.

"Why would you do this to us? There is still time before they get here." I try to reason. "If you loosen up the strap, I'll let you live when I kill everyone."

She ignores me and prepares the table with instruments.

She is older than me, maybe in her thirties. The last time she prepped me for treatment, I saw how her eyes lingered on my torso as she cleaned and shaved me for their experiments. I have witnessed her and the other lab assistants checking out Cortez's body when they were prepping him for so-called treatment when they used to work on us both.

Cortez, Fuck, what they did to Cortez. I hit the back of my head on the metal table, thinking about the events. The action made a loud clanking noise. She drops one scalpel but recovers and aligns it perfectly alongside the instruments on the metal tray.

I lowered my head, not caring that the clasp dug into my neck at the movement. With any luck, I can strangle myself.

Just thinking about Cortez, my body recoiled in reaction to the last time we were together.

"Bright, sit this one out. Another round will kill you." Cortez shoved me to the back of the cell when they came to get me. "I don't think you can make it."

I tried to speak, but my teeth were still chattering from the latest treatment dealing with extreme temperatures, followed by burnings and grafts. I lay back down.

The loud beep buzzes as the cell opens. Cortez stood between me and the four men with long spears that served as tasers.

The night they brought us to the compound, we were able to overtake two men and made it as far as the exit of the building, only to be surrounded by an army of men outside to take us back to the cells.

The enemy captured Cortez and me during our last

mission and sold us to a laboratory that was carrying out disturbing human experiments. Our team is looking for us, but the enemy that sold us is long gone.

These godless people have been killing and experimenting on humans at this camp for years.

"I got it. It doesn't hurt at all," I lie to Cortez while sliding out of the bed and facing the guards. Because of the healing graphs on my side, I couldn't stand at my full height, and the tight scabs made it even more uncomfortable.

"You ain't got shit. Let me do this. You are not going to make this next treatment," he insists.

The guards look puzzled, and the tall blonde, most likely the leader, looks up at the camera. His phone rings, and he speaks to the man in charge in his native language.

Cortez moves closer to me and whispers, "Let me do this. I am working on the girl."

The routine is simple: we are lab rats, and they test our bodies by exposing us to pain, stimuli, and drugs and measuring the effects.

From what we gathered, most of the men who are tested never make it past three months. We are heavily monitored, and the facility houses people from the town who work here and are compensated well for their work. That is what Cortez was able to extract from a village girl.

Cortez charms a village girl who speaks a little English when he is alone with her. He whispers sweet nothing in her ears, hoping she will send word to our team, even Duncan or Donelly, the distress call for the FORECON Recons.

"We have been here for three weeks. We can't last like this. Double over. Faint or some shit. They need to take me, *not you. Bright, you are receiving most of the torture. I can do it this time." His hazel eyes search mine for agreement.*

I nod and double over.

It had been weeks since I had last seen Cortez. When the guards escorted me past one of the glass treatment rooms, I spotted him for the first time since they had taken him in my place.

"Cortez?" I shook my head and blinked, unsure of what I was seeing. The bottom part of his calf is soaked in blue liquid in a tank. I eyed him in horror. He had no legs; they fucking took his legs.

I don't remember what happened next. Although my hands were tied, I must have gone postal. I woke up in my cell, covered with bruises and cracked ribs. They had to wait until I healed to start the treatment.

When they came to retrieve me this morning, I snapped a guard's neck.

If today is the day I will meet my maker, I am not okay with it. I want to set this place ablaze. I miss home. I stare up at the fluorescent light above. I miss my mother.

The drug courses through my veins and I feel it's potency. My heart feels like it is about to explode as my body tenses, trying to break free.

The door to the lab swings open, and I see the scientists pouring into the room with stoic faces. I am not acknowledged as a human being. One of them cranks the table to position it higher.

I face the animals, and then my gaze meets the young lady by the door that Cortez tried to charm. She seems nervous. The men don't see; they are busy reading data.

In the far distance, I spot a hint of compassion on her face, but she looks away as the knife slices, and I growl in pain.

CHAPTER 14 - GAVIN

"We only have a short time. Wake now," the young woman slaps my face. "My English is no good."

The pain is intense; I peer at the pools of blood trickling down my stomach and laugh deliriously.

She reaches for a syringe and jabs into my arm. "It is the only way. Make you strong."

I feel the boost of adrenaline, and I become fully awake as I realize I am completely naked on the table.

She loosens the straps, and I don't wait for them to open. I break free, and on instinct, I put my hand around her neck, ready to snap it.

"Let her go, man. She is on our side," Cortez says, approaching me with what looks like metal sickles serving as legs. He winces as he moves, and pools of sweat run down his face.

I shook my head, trying to speed up my senses and awaken. I eye a scientist on the ground and raise an eyebrow. "Ana injected them with poison," Cortez blurts out with clenched teeth.

I look over to the young lady. "Ana?"

He nods. "Our unit is coming. They should have already been here, but Ana said they planned to take all your parts today. I wanted..."

He didn't finish his thoughts before alarms rang through the lab. Two guards rush into the room.

It was no challenge. I took the taser from one, hit the other one in the throat, and smashed the one overhead, leaving a dent. Pools of blood splashed over the white floors.

Explosions and gunfights came from outside. I stripped one guard and took his pants and shirt.

I look at Cortez. Ana holds him on one side, and he clings to a table for support.

"You can barely stand." I grab him like a rag doll and fling him over my shoulder. We scurry down the hall to another room. I secured him in place and gave him one of the tasers.

"We need weapons," Cortez breathes out.

"Stay here," I command.

"Where are you going?"

"To get the others out."

"Wait for the platoon. Bright, they are here, close, listen." He pauses, breathing through the pain. "The gunfire is subsiding. Stay put."

"Yeah, but this mission is a rescue mission."

"So, what." His brow shoots up.

"They have to pay." I look at Cortez's lower half and blurt out, "All of them."

My mind went to Dante's Inferno and what Virgil and Dante witnessed in the seventh circle of hell.

There are varying punishments for the types of violence committed. Those who commit violence against their neighbors are trapped in a river of boiling blood. *Justice.*

Sensing my thoughts, Cortez blurts out, "Bright, some of these guys are like Ana," he shifts, pain etching his features. "They took the job not knowing what it entailed and only wanted to provide for their families."

"What are you, a fucking Saint?" I open the door and peer down the hall.

Ana let out a small cry. She doesn't understand English, but she understands vengeance.

"You make sure he is okay." I gesture to Ana. I eye Cortez and blurt out before I close the door, "Being poor is no excuse to do what they were doing; I have no sympathy for godless creatures." I lock the door and yell, "I will return for you."

CHAPTER 15 - GAVIN

Present Day:

I sit helpless, in my thoughts betrayed by my confidence that I could protect her. My hands itch to enact Justice.

A chill runs down my spine, imagining what is happening to her. A growl escapes my mouth from the depth of my stomach, just thinking about her lying helpless somewhere. I feel sweat drenching my body.

I count in my head. One, two, three. My breathing is in time with the counting. *Don't fall apart now, Bright. You will find her.*

My thoughts are interrupted by a faint sound. I strain my ears to listen. It sounds like a scratching sound. I look around again, willing the room to give me a clue. *Something. Anything.*

Taking timid steps across the floor, I strain my ears again, and my eyes dart around the room to re-examine the space.

My instincts are the only thing guiding me now, and despite the illogical way my body reacts to the room, there are no threats.

My foot shifts when I hear a faint pop. *It is not my imagination; there is something here.* My senses are on Defcon 1 level alert when I smell a familiar sharp, pungent aroma: a combination of sulfur and charcoal—gunpowder.

Upon instinct, I draw my gun and walk to where the sound came from. It leads me to a stacked pile of rugs. They are too flat to hide anything but carefully arranged to look like they are strewn around. I move one.

It surprises me that it is attached to others and to a panel, sort of like an attic access door, but it is leading underground. When I open it, my eyes widen as I see an entrance to an eighteen-foot-deep room filled with smoke.

Our gazes meet. Diedre is holding a rag around her mouth to protect her from the smoke that she apparently created. She tries to stand, but she winces. She is hurt, and her leg is attached to a shackle.

As she stares up at me, a jolt of relief comes over me as I assess her for injuries. She is hobbling on one leg, one eye is swollen, and her clothing is ripped as she stands barefoot. Relief came first, but now anger boils through my veins.

However, another feeling interrupts my anger. I cannot describe this feeling because I have never felt it before. Anger is replaced by whatever the fuck this feeling is when I see Deidra's face staring up at me, filled with defiance.

CHAPTER 16 – GAVIN

"Don't worry," she says as she sees the end of my gun aiming for the huge guy slumped over the edge of a mattress. "He won't be harming anyone," she grins, causing me to question if she was really a kidnap victim, she continues. "But you can't come down here without a ladder. The other guy took it up." Her voice is cold, and her face and body are calm.

Swiftly, I grab the ladder and carefully lower it down to the room.

Deidra's chains were not long enough for her to guide it in place. Again, I don't follow protocol and let the team know the package is secure. I am losing all sense of normalcy with this woman. I slid down the ladder using the Recon fireman glide and was face-to-face with her in a matter of seconds.

It was natural, and it was my instinct to grab her by the wrist and pull her into me. I hold her to feel her warmth or to make her feel mine. We stand there for minutes in the still-smokey room.

The chilling silence immediately struck me. The walls were padded to create a soundproof, isolationist atmosphere. There was a mattress, refrigerator, sink, and a full bathroom. They were monitoring us in a surveillance area with computer screens highlighting my men's position.

A hidden bunker was not identified in the plans we reviewed repeatedly.

Stan's voice comes through my earpiece, breaking me from her hold. "Sir, we found one. I told the team to take him to the war room but get here quickly because the police have been notified."

I shook my head to ward off the Siren's effects on me and eagerly tried to look at her, but she clung to me.

"I have Ms. Danvers. I found her, but I need a skeleton key or a hacksaw."

"You found her." Stan's voice held elation. "He said he found her." I believe he is telling the team. I hear applause in the background. "You are in the basement?" He questions, undoubtedly tracking my communicator's position.

"Yes," I say. I don't take my gaze off Deidra. She is quiet, just looking at the dead guy in disgust. I continue to talk in my comm. "Are they on the way?"

Deidra put her right hand on my chest. "No, please don't send for anyone," she whispers. "I don't want anyone to see me..." Her gaze goes down to her legs marred with scratches and her bare feet. "Like this."

"Don't bring anyone. I got it," I order while my heart breaks. "We are coming up."

"Gav, there is another guy on the loose." I hear Alex's concerned voice in the comm. I look down at the vomit piece of shit with copious amounts of blood spilled on the mattress and the floor.

"He has been neutralized," I say between clenched teeth.

"But still…" Alex continues.

"Don't fight me on this and take down the cameras for fifteen minutes," I demand.

Alex knows me and knows the tone that means don't fuck with me. "Okay," he relents

"Bring the skeleton key to the war room in twenty minutes." I insist and disable the comm.

"Don't move," I say to Deidra, taking out my Glock, but she shakes her head.

"He has the key in his pants."

I would rather shoot the shackle than touch the loser slumps down on the bed. "It's in his jeans, right pocket," she says with a small exhale.

My hand reaches in and quickly retrieves it. Flashes of a red river coat my head, but I hold it together for her. I took off my jacket and carefully draped it on her.

"Hop on my back; we are climbing up," I say, hunching down so she can hop on.

"Wait." She hesitates as she picks up the rag she used to cover her mouth from the smoke earlier and cleans the bottom of her feet. The shoes she wore earlier, one missing the heel and the other near the mattress, were covered in blood.

I am in disbelief as she carefully wipes the stains off her perfectly manicured toenails. "I don't want to mess up your shirt," she says as if she is reading my mind. "I am ready."

She doesn't want to mess up my shirt, yet her hands are stained with blood. She must be in shock.

I scoot down again as she attempts to hold on. She moans in pain, causing my body to stir in empathy.

"I think I twisted my ankle and can't hold with my left hand," she hesitates. "He dislocated my wrist."

I wish I could kill him again.

I look up at the entrance of the room; there is only one exit. I scoop her up into a fireman's carry and sling her over my shoulder.

"I am sorry, your eye will hurt, but we must do this quickly."

She didn't protest.

The fireman carry is a lifting technique used to rescue someone when time and resources are scarce. Rescuers frequently use it to quickly and safely evacuate the injured person.

Having my team extract her would have been easier, but I understand her. It is not about ego and pride. It is about strength. She is building something, something that has pissed off someone so much that they want to take it away.

Her research centers are a haven for scientists to explore their mission to improve humanity, unlike the ones that want to destroy it. The ones that experimented on humans, on myself and Cortez.

"Clothes," she says when we made it out of the literal hell hole. She tries to stand but collapses, and I hold her. My gaze goes to the red lace bra I tried to suck off her earlier. Heat rises to my face, followed by anger.

"Clothes?" I question.

"I have a change of clothes in my office," she answers. "And I want to take a shower."

"You need a doctor," I reply. I scoop her up like a baby as I carry her to the elevator.

"Thank you," she says in a faint whisper. She looks up at me, her lips upturn in a smile that I guess is only for my benefit.

Her left eye is closed from the swelling, and I try to make my face neutral, trying to hide the sadness and regret that I didn't get to her faster.

"Does it look that bad?" She tries to narrow her eyes but winces.

I bury the anger that is still raging in me.

"Don't worry, you are still beautiful, Siren." I manage to smile.

At this moment, we just need to go to her office, away from spectators. Stall. She can't shower or wash until she sees a doctor and talks to the local authorities, but I won't tell her. Even though it was in self-defense, she killed a person. The police would want a statement.

She buries her face in my chest as if she hears my thoughts. I pretend not to see tears forming in her eyes as the elevator carries us up to the floor where all this madness started—the floor where they took her and where she captivated me.

As the elevator doors open, she points me toward her office. Her head leans close to my chest, and her legs dangle to the side of my left arm.

"I can walk *now.* I am probably too heavy for you," she stammers.

My arms gripped her tighter.

"You are not wearing shoes." I look at her pretty toes, painted a bright pink color but also tarnished with spots of blood from her assailant.

"Let me carry you for now," I say.

I can carry you forever.

CHAPTER 17 – DEIDRA

"The swelling will start going down tomorrow," says the emergency room doctor. His eyes fixed on my left eye, specifically on the swelling that is underneath.

His silver glasses nestle on his nose, and his bushy eyebrow narrows as he gently touches the swollen area, causing me to wince in pain.

"When can I leave?" I blurt out to the doctor. "It's been a long day."

"I don't see why we can't discharge you tonight?" he chuckles at my impatience.

"Really, Deidra?" Irene admonishes.

The doctor nods while taking off his purple latex gloves. "The only thing we need to check is your CT scans to make sure there is no concussion."

I sigh. "How much longer?"

"Deidra?" Irene scolds. "Please, don't."

"Don't chastise me. We've been here for eight long hours." I wave my hand with the IV stuck deep in it. "So, I got punched, strangled, and hit my head, no one di..." My voice trails off. "No one died that didn't need to die."

The doctor puts hand sanitizer on his hands, his face laced with horror. He looks at Irene and nods.

There is no acknowledgment of the murderer, I guess. I don't blame him. I want to go home to hide, bury myself in my bedroom, and cry.

"The beeping of the monitors and the hospital lighting have me on edge. Irene, please go home. I am fine," I plead.

"Unfortunately, your sister won't be able to make it until Wednesday."

Recalling my conversation with my sister earlier broke my heart. I promised her I was okay, but she and my nephew wanted to come to see for themselves. I lied to her to get her off the phone. There is no way I will allow her up here.

And since I am good at telling white lies...

"Irene, I've hired a home health care worker to stay with me. She is at the house now." I lie to my assistant and my friend.

I have vivid memories of when she came up to my office and saw me, how she ran to me and hugged me as if I had come back from the land of the dead.

"When did you have time to do this?" Her words come out skeptical.

"I don't know," I shrug. "Maybe when you were checking on Bobby or when you were in the cafeteria when the police were questioning me?"

She squints at me to assess if I am bluffing.

"Why did the doctor look at me like I punch babies for a living?" I questioned, trying to change the subject so that she didn't have time to verify my lie. "Bobby could have died from his injuries. Tell me what his wife said again."

"She *said* that she hopes our worker's comp is intact because her husband is not returning to work for Danvers Lab."

"Yikes!" I fake giggle.

"You just tried to change the subject, didn't you?" Irene's lips curve into a smile.

"Guilty. You know that the ABC Agency has a man guarding me."

Irene's gaze went to the door of the room. She informed me earlier that the guard was a beefy, no-nonsense guard who scowled at everyone coming close to the room. I concealed my disappointment when Gavin left with the police detective earlier.

"You mean to say the D.B.C," she corrects me.

I try to laugh at my joke, but she ignores my humor.

Spotting her mind working overtime, I continue to convince her.

"Stan is going to take you home as well." I sit up in the bed, my head feeling heavy with the swelling, waiting for the opportunity to tell her she is only going home to pack. I place the ice pack on my face.

"Irene, you are the only person close to me for the

past seven years." Tears blur my vision, but I hold them at bay. "I don't want to fire you to protect you, but if you insist on staying close to me, I will."

"Why didn't you think I would leave, like some analysts did?" She narrows her eyes and gives me a steely stare.

"I know you," I smooth out my hospital gown. "You are loyal, and I love you for that. I need you to be safe, and I need you to go with the guard. He is taking you to the safe house."

"Safe house?" she repeats.

"If you want to call it that, it is a five-star hotel suite." I chuckle.

"When did you know? And why are you just now telling me?"

"I knew you wouldn't leave until they discharged me, but I am going to be fine." I remove the ice pack. "Please trust me, Irene. You've done so much already, you've canceled appointments, got me a new phone," my voice goes low. "I can't focus on me or the company while worrying about your safety."

Her soft nod indicates that she understands. "You are planning to tell Bernie not to come?"

She knows me too well. I only agreed to have my sister and nephew come to shut Bernie up. There is no way I will let her and my nephew partake in this dumpster fire that my life has become.

"I will soon," I tell her the truth.

She inhales and releases tears. The second time today, I saw tears I was responsible for inflicting on my friend, causing me to release the tears I was fighting to keep at bay.

We quickly wipe the tears away when we hear a knock at the door.

"Enter," I say, clearing my throat.

Disappointment hung in the space when Stan entered the room.

Where is Gavin? Why did he leave after the detective took my statement?

"Ms. Cummings?" Stan, the tall, lean security specialist, motions to Irene.

I guess a requirement to work at the security firm is you have to be insanely attractive.

She nods and hugs me. Before she exits, the reluctant look on her face reminds me of movies in which a dutiful soldier leaves a comrade alone on the battlefield.

As soon as they leave, I collapse back onto the small hospital bed.

My mind is carefully going over the details I shared with the detective about my short-lived kidnapping. Not that I worry I did something wrong, but I wonder why my protector, Gavin Bright, exited stage left as soon as the detective finished questioning me. *He has been gone most of the day.*

I close my eyes to concentrate, hoping to relive the activities so I can be as accurate as possible when the gritty detective grilled me on the events leading up to my kidnapping, which the local police station already had our complaints on file months ago. Yet, they couldn't develop any leads or movement on the case.

Detective Rick Strickner seemed more interested in how my kidnapper met his demise than what really happened.

He demanded that I recount the harrowing incident near the elevator, detailing the moment the failed rapist choked me and groped me, mentioning the button I had left as a clue. Gavin's face was neutral. He stood by the window away from the questioning, taking notes.

I informed the detective about waking up in a construction bin. Before they took me out, I left another button ripped from my lab coat. Moreover, I stumbled upon the soon-to-be notorious murder weapon - a lengthy, brittle wall nail that I cunningly wedged into the waist of my form-fitting skirt.

"What did you think leaving buttons around would accomplish?" The detective inquired, causing me to tilt my head to the side in annoyance.

He was more focused on buttons than on how lucky I was that there was something I could use to free myself after being shoved in the construction supply bin and wheeled around like garbage.

"Duh," I said to the now bewildered detective. "I intentionally left clues to alert the security team that I had been abducted and was still somewhere in the building." I couldn't resist using the word 'Duh'; that word was what my nephew Ben always used when something was obvious.

"The forensic team found the so-called murder weapon at the foot of the mattress," I recall the detective's voice being filled with doubt.

He went over the details of how I used the thick, long nail to pierce the neck of my assailant, hitting a major artery.

"Did you think of any other alternative?" The detective's face held contempt, and his lip was straight, with no hint of compassion.

"Detective, the vile brute ripped my panties, hiked up my skirt, ground his limp dick on me, and told me that if I moved, he would finish the job he started earlier of choking me and fuck my dead caucus." I look into his startled blue eyes with dark circles accompanying his pale face.

Observing, Gavin chose to look out the window instead of paying attention to the harsh questioning. My frustrations got the better of me.

I continue, "It sounds like you would rather interrogate me, but I survived the mother fucker's attack, the same motherfucker that crept my assistant and me out months ago. So much so, I fired him."

The monitor started to beep. I looked at it because the beeping became louder, and I calmed myself with deep breaths.

"Listen, the last thing I wanted was to cause harm to anyone, much less kill someone. I just wanted to live."

The monitor's alarm also startled Gavin because he turned to look at the device but not at me.

When the detective politely nodded at me after the

nurses came in, Gavin exited with him.

Did Gavin leave because he didn't like my brattish behavior? Or did the fact that the detective labeled me a murderer disgust him?

I place the eye pack on my eye when I lie on my right side, feeling satisfied that the nurse pulled out the IV and that I did not have to hold it up. It is sitting nicely on my face.

The cold ice pack dulls the pain. Earlier, the doctor suggested sedatives to help me rest, but I didn't want to dull my senses.

What is taking so long for my discharge to complete? Oh well, it is not like anyone is waiting for me at home. Even Gavin abandoned me. I am used to people leaving. I haven't seen him or heard from him in hours. The additional guard introduced himself when Gavin left. Gavin didn't even say goodbye.

Perhaps I should welcome sleep. I am tired, so tired.

"You fucking bitch! You think you are so smart with your dumb words?" His bad breath is close to my face, and his dry, stringy, long blonde hair feels like straw on my cheek.

"How can words be dumb? The people speaking them control the words." I say to him, "So aren't people the dumb ones?" But the anger flashes in his eyes, proving he doesn't like my dumb words.

Looks like I have to fight this bastard off in my dreams, too.

CHAPTER 18 – GAVIN

"How can words be dumb?" Standing at the foot of the hospital bed, I hear Deidra whimper those words in her sleep. Amusement at her words gave me a sense of relief.

Is she going to be okay? Will she suffer memories she can't control?

Pushing the thoughts down, I stand at the side of her bed in the dark hospital room. The light from the streetlights shone through the window and cast shadows on her profile. I feel like the embodiment of Erik in Gaston Leroux's novel, The Phantom of the Opera. She is my Christine. *I am becoming obsessed with her.*

Her curly hair fans out on the pillow, her eyebrows arch, animated with every sound she makes. I frown when my gaze shifts to the nasty bruises around her eye. That animal wanted to take away her spirit. He was a disturbed soul that needed to be dealt with decisively, and she did the world a favor.

His extensive criminal record included a five-year prison sentence for the heinous crime of rape with malicious wounding, along with felony possession of a firearm and other offenses, was more than enough to garner his execution.

I've killed more men who didn't do half the evil deeds he did, all in the spirit of war, protecting my country, and justice well served. Yet, where was I when she needed protecting?

My frown grows deeper, recalling her words when she told the detective what the assailant did to her and tried to do to her. I had to look somewhere else to hide my festering anger boiling to the surface. Anger so hot I had to bite the inside of my jaw to control myself, so I looked out the window.

The detective informed me that the district attorney had no interest in pressing charges. Still, Deidra needed to report to the detective in a few days to answer questions and make a statement against the other assailant.

Thanks to Duncan's connections, I was granted the opportunity to visit the other scum bag assailant in custody and see him face-to-face. I had to hurry to the station before they processed him to go to the county jail.

I hauled ass to downtown Fairfax, leaving Alex and Stan to do background and tie things together with all the players we now knew. Not saying goodbye to my Siren was not what I wanted to do. Subconsciously. I didn't know what to say, so I awkwardly left the room with the Detective.

Calvin Walker, the scumbag, did a two-year stint with the dead guy and claimed that Bobby, the guard, was supposed to be knocked out with chlorophyll, a potent compound that, when inhaled, makes someone go unconscious. However, he fought, and the stabbing was an accident.

Tears stream down the perp's face, and snot falls from his nose to his mouth since his hands are tightly cuffed to the table.

"Listen, man, I was told we were only going to keep her for a week in the bunker, but Lou got violent. He said he owed Ms. Danvers some payback for firing him." He hangs his head down. "I promise, man. I promise they told me no one was going to get hurt."

"Is there a way to contact the person who wanted you to keep Ms. Danvers?" I ask, desperately wanting to slug him, but I keep my voice neutral.

Silence hung in the room, causing him to do all the talking between sobs.

The captain and the lead detective agree with our team completely. They understand that our sole opportunity to get closer to the person bent on destroying the new Danvers Research Center is to use Calvin as bait.

Some of our best guys and members of the police department are with him now in a safe house condo in D.C.

Earlier, he made the call to a guy who orchestrated the kidnapping, pretending to escape.

We listen as the call is recorded and traced in the other room while Calvin talks in a deep, ominous voice.

"My client and I paid a lot of money to have her out of commission." His breath sounded heavy like he was overweight. "Too bad you guys couldn't finish the job. We have been planning this for months. What do you want from me? The job is not done."

The detective coaches Calvin and writes on a pad, pointing the words out.

"Well, at least she will be out of commission for a few weeks. Lou clocked her good in the eye. I tried to stop him, but he told me to leave because the guard made me."

There was laughter on the line, causing me to tighten my fists.

"She won't be meeting the SEC in a few days, that's for sure. Too bad he didn't kill the bitch, but I will take that."

Anger rages in my body. *They don't want the company to go public, so I coach Calvin on* what to say.

"I need money to get out of here," he hesitates. "I need to get out of the city."

"That's your problem." The angry voice echoes through the phone

Calvin's eyes widen when he reads what the detective writes and says it out loud.

"If you don't pay me, I will go straight to the cops. They are looking for me, anyway."

There was a moment of silence. "Alright, I'll be there in a few days," he agrees. "Where are you staying?"

The detective's hand's motion, no, the same as mine.

"I can't tell you. I will let you know when you

are in town." Calvin reads the note. "Can't you come tomorrow?"

"Okay, but don't contact me until I call you when I am there." He hisses and hangs up.

The line went dead. The guy with glasses and the awful comb-over, the professional tracer, entered the room, nodding to show the thumbs-up sign. I have already received confirmation from Stan that he received the address as well.

"The guy on the line was the only guy you have dealt with?" I ask Calvin.

He nods. "Why would he come all the way from Denver to give me money?"

Detective Randell answers. "He is not only coming to give money. I bet he is also sending a hit squad to keep you quiet."

Calvin's hands tremble. "But I don't know nothing."

"They think you do." We all turn to the voice in the shadows. My gaze meets Mike, who will be one of my men staying overnight to guard the bait.

I turn my attention to Johnny, the detective who has ties to Duncan, who will guard Calvin, and Mike, who will stand guard outside the building.

"Inform me when you gain the name of the person the address is registered to."

Johnny nods.

I shake the detective's hand and head to the hospital.

On my way here, the fellas, Alex and Duncan, help me assemble the pieces. They already have a lead on the person in Colorado; it turns out he owns an interest in the second-largest research center in the USA.

"It sounds like these clowns don't want her to take the company public," Alex explains, his voice booming through the Bluetooth of my Rover.

"Yeah, if you miss the invitation, you won't be able to officially reschedule the meeting with the SEC for another year, and they might not agree to the meeting," Duncan chimes in and continues. "I am almost finished with the Senator; I will wrap up tomorrow. Why don't I stay in your guest house and help you protect your woman?"

"She is not my woman."

Both Duncan and Alex echo in unison. "Yet."

"She could have died," I murmur, gripping the steering wheel. I can't get to the hospital fast enough.

"But she didn't," Duncan blurts out. "Stan told me she shish kebabbed that motherfucker that put his hands on her. I like her already. Let me know if she has a sister." Duncan laughs.

"What happened to the Senator's daughter who locked herself in your room half naked?" Alex asks. Then, he went on without Duncan answering him. "You go through women more than Gavin goes through novels."

"It's called reading. My mother is a retired high school English teacher. Reading is..."

After telling them for the hundredth time, it finally clicked in my mind — my brothers were distracting me, trying to make sure that I was mentally prepared before encountering Deidra. The hard part is coming; she will have to deal with the trauma of what she did.

"Guys, I know what you are doing. It's something I can handle. Earlier today, I saw the bruises on her neck and the swelling of the eye. She is tough." I say with resolve. "I am good."

"Duncan will join us when he gets in tomorrow morning," Alex adds. "We are close; we will wrap this case up quickly."

As I wrestle with the day's events, I hear my Siren whimper behind me, bringing me out of my contemplations and away from the moon that came out to keep me company as the long day whines down in my head.

Before I looked at her for some time as she slept, I came to take her home but didn't want to wake her because she seemed to be resting comfortably.

"Mommy? Where are you?" She cries. "I can't see you, Mommy." She trashes around in the bed, and a fine mist of perspiration forms on her forehead. "No, No, No, No, Mommy, No."

All I can do is lightly shake her.

Am I supposed to shake her when she is having a

nightmare or a night terror? What do I do?

I press the call button for the nurses' station.

"Don't leave me, Mommy. I have to fight everyone alone. The big oaf is coming, Mommy, don't leave me."

My heart breaks again as I hold her through screams and tears.

"Deidra, wake up, baby. You don't have to fight anyone alone anymore. I am here." My voice was low, a faint whisper in her ears. "Siren, I am here."

As she looks up at me, skepticism fills her eyes before she squints and finally opens them fully. Her bloodshot eye catches my attention but still meets my gaze. Tears wet her long lashes.

"Gavin, is that you? Is it really you, Gavin? You didn't leave me? You don't think I am a brat, a murderer?" She sobs.

I shake my head no while I position my body under hers and hold her in my arms. The tiny hospital bed didn't feel so tiny.

When I was five years old, the bullies on the block took my favorite toy, my big wheel trike, which I was so proud of riding up and down the block. I didn't cry. Upon hearing my mother's words about my daddy not returning from Afghanistan, a mixture of anger and sadness welled up inside me, yet I remained dry-eyed. No tears. When my mother got sick and when I lost some of my comrades and witnessed the brutal torture of my best friend, causing him to lose both legs, I remained stoic. No tears.

Tears now bite at my eyes. When she nuzzles closer to me, her body shutters from the sobs.

This lady witnessed her mother's suicide from the end of a rope. She spent a year in foster care because her father didn't want to claim her. She went to college on a scholarship and took care of her half-sister after she divorced and when her father disowned her for getting pregnant. She is the epitome of strength. Her breakdown guts me.

I wave away the nurses who opened the door to peek in. Their mouths agape, and they walk backward out the door.

Deidra clings to me as I hold her in a vice grip, rocking back and forth as I have her now.

"Don't let me go, Gavin. Please hold me tighter," she begs. "There was so much blood."

A raspy and pained voice, which I think is mine, answers her. "I should have been there to protect you. I am sorry."

As her body trembles on mine, tears flow down my face.

"Tears are pain leaving the spirit." Cortez's voice reverberates, *"Man, if you don't cry, you can't heal. Let that shit go."*

And just like that, this siren has me crying like a baby fresh out of the womb. I cry for growing up missing my father. For not being home, stuck with secret missions when my mother battled breast cancer. I cry, and I cry for the people I lost and the poor guys I killed in the name of duty. I cry for what they did to me and Cortez in that lab and what I did to them. I cry for my Siren.

Together, we cry. Together, we will heal.

CHAPTER 19 – DEIDRA

"There, how does it look now?" I ask my sister on FaceTime, holding my cell phone close to my eye. "Does this concealer look better?"

"I wouldn't say it looks better," Bernie says as she squints while tilting her head to the side. "It looks like you are trying to conceal a black eye. "Haha," I fake laugh while going to the closet to show her the outfit I will wear in a few days for the meeting with the SEC liaisons. I continue, "Well, we put together a well-rehearse plan this morning, and I am doing my part to prepare for the event that is taking place the day after tomorrow."

"We?" I turn to see her arch eyebrow and animated inquiry.

"Gavin and his team." The truth is that every time I utter Gavin's name or think about him, my heart beats at an alarming pace.

"Hmm, Gavin." She stretches out his name and says in a teasing tone. "Do you want to share this elaborate plan with me?"

I snicker and tell her the details of what the team concocted this morning—the plan or how the B.D. Cortez's security and protection team worked with me to implement it.

"Come on, Sis, the plan is not that bad," I insist when I see her eyes glazing over. I pet Kevin and move him to the side.

Gavin and Kevin, my sweet cat, insisted that they would not leave my side when Gavin brought me home late last night. Kevin slept in my room, while Gavin slept in the guest room down the hall.

The way he held me in the hospital bed, the way he carried me bridle-style up the stairs, refusing to put me down. The night we sat on my sofa and talked. I sat in his lap and talked until morning.

"So, you are just going to tell the SEC representative that you have a severe allergic reaction to pollen and wear your shades during the meeting?" Bernie inquires, waking me from my thoughts

"Yeah. "I retort, "Duncan came up with that one, and Alex said that if more than two people agree to a lie, folks new to the conversation will believe it's true."

"Who are Alex and Duncan?" she asks.

"They are close friends and partners." I furrow my brow, trying to recall who is who in the dynamic. "I swear, Bernie, it is like you have to be tall and good-looking to work for this company. Duncan doesn't want to be a partner but has *all* these connections. He found the building where we will meet the SEC team on Thursday since the police have our office on lockdown."

I saw them on the Zoom screen, with all the parties and accomplices to the plan, even Irene. However, Gavin claimed there was something wrong with his camera, and we were offline so that they couldn't see me.

I can see how he protected me. He knew I didn't want anyone to see my bruised face.

She puts her index finger on her chin, indicating she is in deep thought. She has done this ever since she was a little girl.

"Let me get this straight: the SEC people will still meet you and don't know what happened yesterday." She arches her brow. I mean the whole incident, the um, um.."

"The fucker that kidnapped me, and what happened to him? Yeah, they don't know. The guys kept it out of the headlines. They are holding one of the accomplices; from what I understand, it all goes down later today." I hiss, finishing Bernie's sentence.

"You are so strong. I am so proud of you." Her smile instantly relaxes me.

"Thank you, sis. You motivate me to be better." I sigh and take a deep breath. "Bernie, if the company becomes public, it will do so much for the cause of our research." She nods, and I add, "And we can relax a bit, having more protocols to protect our legacy."

My cell phone rings, interrupting Facetime.

"Do you have to take that?"

I shake my head. "It is the HOA's management company reminding me that the voting will occur in one month. I missed the debates last night, but they assured me that I am still in the running."

"Deidra, I worry about you. You have so much on your plate, yet you are seeking vengeance on a HOA because of the sins of our father. They dismissed you, and you are going all scorched earth on them. Am I right?" She sighs.

"You are partly right but a bit wrong." I set the phone on my dresser, giving her a full view of the room so she could see the outfit I was trying on.

"How can I be wrong and right at the same time?" She questions, raising her brow.

"You are right. I punished our father not for his neglect toward me and his ability to expand the company handed to him but for how he treated my mother, the most vibrant young scientist." The memories I try to repress come rushing back. "He broke her with empty promises," I smile as I state, "but it is her name that is on the company that is going public. He used her and discarded her like expired milk. He had to pay. What he did to you, a person he claimed to love so much that he brought *me* to his wife's house to cheer you up after your mom died of cancer, was beyond dreadful."

I slip into the dress I plan to wear to the meeting and continue my speech.

"Our father was justice well served." I glimpse Bernie's nod in agreement. "You are not right about me going all scorched earth on the Homeowners Association. The HOA's management provides a service to homeowners. They dismissed my claims about the weed spraying and told me I did not warrant making suggestions as if I were not a homeowner. The pesticides have ingredients that have been proven to cause cancer. When I win, I will fire them for neglect. It's about understanding and using resources to protect people, which are given to them freely."

"I am still working on my PhD, and after all that, I still don't understand the difference." She shakes her head, her beautiful honey eyes gleaming with glee.

"When you get your PHD, then maybe you will." I gave her a sly smile.

We break out in laughter.

I move toward the phone so my sister can approve the form-fitting bright red dress with a modest boatneck neckline.

"Oh my." She clasps her hands together. "Deidra, you look absolutely stunning. And it *does* take away from your eye."

My body stiffens when a deep voice clears his throat behind me. *Gavin.*

"I didn't mean to interrupt you." He steps in, sees my sister's face on the screen, and mimics holding his heart. "I thought you were talking to yourself. Stan wants to go over some more details with Irene since she will be at the meeting on Thursday. Can you make it into your den office in thirty minutes?" he asks.

"Yes, I, um, will be there, and this is my, um, rittle, I mean little sister on the phone."

Fuck, my mouth is dry, and it feels like I swallowed a giant watermelon, and it is lodged in my throat when he is around. Get it together... Did I say rittle sister? I am intelligent, classy, and charming.

"Bernie," my sister says. "I am Bernie, Deidra's rittle sister," she giggles. "Seriously, thank you for taking care of her. On the surface, she comes off as an ardent grizzly bear, but she is a softie once you get to know her."

Kevin goes to Gavin to steal all the attention and plops before him for a belly rub. Gavin rubs him, looks at Bernie, and responds, "I know, and I will."

"Hey, I'm in the room. Don't talk like I am not here."

Okay, show them that you are not frazzled.

"Do you like my outfit?" I do a complete spin and bend down to rub Kevin's belly as well. "You told me to wear something bright to differentiate myself from the others so the team can spot me easily and also take away from my eye." I do another spin. "You like?"

His silver eyes went dark. He nods and picks up Kevin.

"Let's go, boy. Let them have their ladies' time. Drake is downstairs; I am leaving to meet the team for the mission. I won't be there for the meeting with Stan and Irene. See you tonight, and it was nice meeting you, Bernie."

I close the door, turn back to Bernie, and frown.

"Oh my God," Bernie fawns. "He is so dreamy, tall, muscular, and those eyes." She covers her mouth. "I can see why you chose to hump him in the conference room."

I sigh while wiggling out of the red number. "He probably doesn't see me with much interest anymore."

"Why would you say that?"

Because he saw my pathetic crying ass and maybe thought I was a messy problem he couldn't afford to solve. I tried kissing him on the couch when we talked all the way in the morning, but he pulled away. I list all the reasons why in my head.

"Where did you go just now?"

"Nowhere," I shrug. "Gavin is not interested in someone like me."

"Girl, when you bent down to rub that dreadful cat of yours, his flag was at full attention." She laughs. "He took the cat to cover his crotch."

"Why are you looking at his crotch?" I question, but I feel a weight lifting as I giggle.

"It was in the direct proximity of my gaze. I can't see the whole room, but I can see a guy that tall, his midsection, and sis, he is packing." She laughs heartedly. "Trust and believe if these guys are as fine as you say. I can't wait to meet them."

"All, Bernie, I mean *all* of the guys are HOT; the Duncan guy has the bluest eyes I have ever seen, next to my nephew. Also, when he came close to the screen, I saw one eye had the same genetic defect as Ben's. There is a brown triangle part at the blue." I state with enthusiasm, now holding the phone close to see her reaction.

"Hmm, Duncan," she shakes her head. "His father's

name is Benjamin, and he was sure he was doing twenty years in the military. However, I wouldn't mind meeting this Duncan fellow."

I smile at my younger sister as she makes fun of me for not being able to speak when Gavin is in the room. As she shares more stories about Ben, my smile grows wider, and I feel a sense of normalcy once more.

The worries about the *mission* Gavin and his team are conducting on my behalf disappear.

CHAPTER 20 – GAVIN

Calming and inviting are two words I would use to describe Deidra's home. It's hard to believe that she completed all the intricate painting designs and accents representing her personality in just three months.

Sitting in the breakfast nook, I can't help but admire the carefully chosen color palette. The soft, romantic colors of lilac and cream, with a subtle hint of pink, can be found throughout the home.

As I reminisce about the first time we met, a smile plays on my lips. I remember how she marveled at my furnishings, recognizing the same drapes and chair upholstery designers. It's clear now that she was admiring our similar tastes.

Honestly, I envy the intricate moldings and delicate nature-inspired motifs strategically placed throughout the main level to collect light and lend an air of sophistication and comfort.

My siren has excellent taste. Also, if I am honest with myself, this is the first time I feel this level of comfort in someone else's space.

I take a sip of the Merlot, which she must have opened earlier with her meal. With every sip, the wine gradually relaxes the tension built up throughout the day.

As I stare out the window, I notice the night sky reveals a crescent moon, casting a soft glow on the surroundings, while the shimmering stars add a touch of mystery to the evening. Behind two majestic oak trees, a small hot tub beckoned to my soar body to come to soak; it is nestled amidst a lush green canopy, creating a romantic oasis.

Upon my arrival, I hastily dismissed the additional guards. Before, I went to my house, desperate for a refreshing shower and a change of clothes. I have been sitting here for the past hour thinking about her. The verses of Lord Byron's poem, "She Walks in Beauty," echo through my mind.

Relief washes over my body because now I know she is safe. My ears strain to hear her, but all I hear is the hum of the kitchen appliances. I look down at my watch. It is only 10 pm.

My siren must have gone to bed. All the best. No telling if I can control myself.

The team did well today, even though I was sloppy. My mistake could have been drastic if I had not been wearing my vest.

I reminisce about seeing Alex emerge from retirement from the desk in fully detailed SWAT gear and run through the streets of a neighborhood in Maryland.

Still, it was Duncan's goofy ass that got me to laugh out loud in the empty kitchen when I remember those angry blue eyes staring intently at me with his palms up, shaking his head, disappointed that the mission was over too quickly.

I laugh out loud again when remembering that Duncan flung the perp over his shoulder like a rag doll after Alex bound his hands and mouth. "You are going to pay for not making me work harder," Duncan shouts.

"What is so funny?" The Siren asks, causing me to sit up straight quickly, feeling as guilty as a child caught red-handed with forbidden cookies.

"You didn't go to bed?" Moving down on the bench, I question, willing her to sit beside me.

She takes the bait and sits right next to me. My body buzzes with excitement.

"Go to bed?" she questions. "While you are out there risking your life. I did fall asleep a bit," she chuckles. "I ordered Ethiopian food earlier; I made you a plate. Did you eat?"

My eyes widen with the news. She remembered that I confessed that I often eat at the Ethiopian food place off Highway 50.

I swallow the lump in my throat. "I am not hungry, but wine will suffice for now. Thank you."

Her hair was slicked back tight in one of those stretching clips Kevin used to bring me. My hands itch to release those strands and run my fingers through her long tresses. Her face was fresh, smooth, and without makeup. *I want to kiss her.*

I can't help but frown when I see the hints of

purple and pink around her left eye, but I take comfort in seeing the swelling going down. The red only shows when she turns her eyes to the left. Her inviting, rich brown skin tempts me to reach out and discover if it's as velvety as it appears. She is wearing a long Yankees night shirt, its blue fabric complementing her skin.

When I brought her home that night, I found out that she loves baseball. I could see the excitement in her eyes as we talked about the game. Neither one of us was sleepy. We stayed on the sofa all night talking while I held her. However, when she leaned in to kiss me, I backed away. I couldn't risk her siren moves jeopardizing her life. I promised Alex not to mix business with pleasure; besides, I wanted to focus on what we completed today.

"Soooo," she says drawing out the word to break up the awkward silence and to bring me out of my contemplations. "Are you going to tell me why you are laughing out loud in the dark by yourself?"

"My apologies." I don't know why, but I put my hand over hers. "I thought you were sleeping?"

Her body stiffens under my touch, yet she defiantly pretends that my touch does not affect her.

She furrows her brow. "It went well then?" She tries to read my face to gauge.

I nod. "Extremely well. The hardest part was getting the detective out of the way." When our eyes met, I felt an irresistible urge to move closer, enticed by the depth and warmth of her brown eyes. I shake my head to continue my words. "However, we eluded him and have the mark captive."

"Captive?" She knits her brows. "You have the guy that ordered to kidnap me captive?"

I nod, "I would extract the information myself, but Alex and Duncan felt I wouldn't be able to control myself." I clear my throat. "Considering how close I am to the client."

Her index finger points to her chest while she smirks. "Little old me." Her eyes are wide as she exaggerates her words.

Yes, you, Siren, I can't get enough of you. I want you on me like last night on the sofa, whispering nonsense but everything to each other.

Even though our legs are touching, I scoop her up to sit on my lap.

"Oh," She giggles with a startled look. My nostrils flare to inhale her fragrant scent of honeysuckles, the sweet-smelling flower that lined our walkway to the front door of my childhood home in Kentucky.

Thump! The loud sound Kevin makes, leaping on the table to interrupt me as I lean in to kiss her.

"Kevin, you cock blocker," my Siren scolds, causing me to laugh harder but wince a bit when Deidra's elbow catches my rib.

"What is it?" She cries with an arch brow.

Without waiting for an answer, she hastily rolls up my Henly to examine the bruise caused by a bullet that my Teflon vest prevented. Her eyes are as big as saucers. "From today?"

"My head was in the game, I promise, but I didn't anticipate that one of the guys hid behind a car with a 22."

Her fingers trace the bruise. She moves my shirt up more to examine my tattoos; her mouth reads the words of my poetry written for a man I love. I twist my body when her fingers go further to explore the space further up my ribs; I didn't want her to see.

My twisting action startles her when I pull away, thinking it is because of something else.

She whispers, "Who is Martin?" Confusion shows on her face.

I couldn't help but softly chuckle at her hesitancy. "Just the most important man I have ever known," I tease.

She hops out of my lap. "I see." She tilts her head to the side.

My laughter fills the kitchen. I move up the Henly for her to read all the words etched up my right rib cage.

"All the lessons and the deeds, even in your absence, you guide me," she reads as her fingers trace the words.

"Martin Gavin Bright," I answer her unasked question, reaching for her hand. "My father."

She tries to hit me, and I believe she is pretending she wants to walk away, but I catch up to her before she leaves the kitchen, holding her waist from behind.

I turn her to face me, and I can see her face is flush and her breathing is labored.

My Siren wants me, too.

"You tease too much," she huffs.

"No, my Siren, you are the tease." I run my fingers along her jawline. "I still haven't seen the polka dot bottoms of the suit you took from me."

She rolls those mysterious brown eyes of hers.

"Those are *my* bottoms that Kevin temporarily gifted to you."

Her seductive smile fills the room with desire. She fiddles with her hair and raises her brows.

"Start up the hot tub," she says with a sly smile. I will meet you out there." With a hop in her step, she joyfully skips away, her excitement contagious as Kevin follows her close behind.

The jacuzzi jets come to life, giving the water jets power as the temperature slowly rises. Hearing the rhythmic sensation of the water as it forces streams creates a soothing experience. My mood is calm.

I carefully set the wine and a tray of snacks on the counter near the tub. I can't recall a time when I felt so relaxed and hopeful. I was never eager for relationships and wasn't the one to fall into anything.

The fellas often remind me I am not the type to settle down because I am always on. My brain constantly works on a series of threats, some real and some made up.

My cell phone buzzes. Glancing at the screen to see Duncan's number, my excitement grows, and I almost drop the phone while swiping to answer.

I place Alex and Duncan on speaker.

Please tell me that this ends tonight.

"He sang like the proverbial canary," chuckles Duncan. "It was disappointing that I couldn't showcase my expertise more."

My mind flashes to Duncan's knife skills, but Alex's interruption shortens Duncan's unenthusiastic rant.

"Danvers Research Facility put Laban's Labs out of business. Alan Holms owns the holding company," Alex informs.

"Alan Holms?" I question. "His name rings a bell."

"It should," Duncan interjects. "He attended grad school with your woman. She was engaged to him but broke off the engagement to start her own research."

"Yeah, yeah–I know about him. Are you serious? He put this whole thing on because she jilted him?"

"Among other things," Alex explains. "Eight years ago, he assumed the position of CEO, but his decision-making skills resulted in a series of detrimental business choices."

"He partnered with Deidra's former business competitor. That guy was the mastermind behind the two-bit hitman squad. Apparently, Alan contacted him and financed the team up for payback. Which adds up to the address we trace the call to." Duncan adds.

Alex sighs. "The goal was to prevent the SEC approval and keep her in the space they created, but the Marc guy lost his livelihood and was out for revenge."

"This Alan tool has been bleeding money since he took over the company. Several competitive labs and supply companies are under his ownership and have all reaped the rewards of the labs' ancillary services. Still, if Danvers' goes public, the chance of recovery is slim." Alex explains. "Basically, Danvers is on the verge of burying him and the competition in the field."

"We are going to give the ringleader to the cops. He will probably cut a deal to squeal on Alan." Duncan chimes in.

"This mother fucker has to pay the price for messing with her. No one will ever touch her again, you hear me? I am protecting her from now on."

Maybe forever if she lets me.

"Let him cut the deal and wait for it to play out, but his days are numbered," I growled in the phone so loud that the crickets stopped chirping.

"Chill out. We are on your side," Alex says, then shifts the conversation. "Gavin, you took one. If you were not wearing a vest, you could have..." His voice goes low.

"But it didn't. Force Recon prevailed today." Duncan adds.

"Neat bow?" I ask. In Recon, there's a term to describe the last step of tying everything together to ensure the desired outcome is achieved.

"Yeah, neat bow." Alex agrees.

"Guys," I say, starting to thank them.

"Shut the fuck up." Duncan interrupts. "We didn't

break a sweat. Now, handle your business with your woman."

I can picture Alex rolling his eyes. "Hey, we are tying it up," he says. "She meets with the SEC on Thursday, so you have a day to–" he pauses, "Relax."

"Relax? Man, you better do more than relax, if you know what I mean." Duncan chortles.

I cut him off. "Thanks, good night."

I hang up on Duncan, still saying crude things about how good the night can be.

Shedding my shirt and jeans, I eagerly slide into the inviting tub, feeling the soothing water envelop my body.

The clear night sky adds a touch of magic to the secluded section of the garden, making it the perfect romantic spot for a rendezvous, but it has been some time since she went to put on her swimsuit.

Suppose we've missed something?

Panic rushes through my body as I get up in a rush and head to her room, only to find her closed bedroom door. It's locked. I knock.

"Go away." The voice says, not sounding like her. *She is crying.*

I kick open the door to find her in her polka-dot swimsuit, holding Kevin and weeping.

My Siren is gorgeous, even with a black eye and tears. I hitch my breath.

"What is it?"

She points to the intercom system. I automatically know what she is referring to. I have one in my bedroom and throughout the house to hear and to alert guests.

"I didn't mean to eavesdrop. I was calling to let you know I would be down soon." She put Kevin down and brought her knees up to her chest.

Does she not know she is in the tiniest bikini?

My eyes are feasting on the treat before me as my mouth waters. I try to speak. "I am sorry. I was going to tell you later tonight, maybe tomorrow morning."

With a subtle nod of her head, she signals she agrees. I drop to my knees on the soft, white, plush carpet that perfectly complements the delicate pastel patterns of her room.

"Don't cry for that bastard." I fist my hair and search her eyes. "Do you still have a thing for him?"

She looks up to the ceiling and shakes her head.

"It's you," she says, wiping her cheeks as I cup her face. "No one's ever..." she closes her eyes, fighting to get the words out. "I thought you didn't like me like that, but what you said about protecting me?"

I grapple with the feeling tightening in my chest. "I have to confess, it's all true." Looking up at her, I add, "I backed away yesterday because I needed complete concentration on what we were focusing on today."

I pull her legs out to dangle on the side of the bed. The feel of her smooth tone skin has my cock springing up underneath the towel. Reaching up, I kiss her. I taste her. She moans as I deepen the kiss. Our tongues delight each other in a dance. However, I need more. I reach for her bikini and slide my index finger to part her folds. Smooth and slippery.

My breath is heavy with anticipation when I feel how tight and wet her pussy is. *She is ready for me.* Her smooth slit is inviting, and my mind is lost. This remarkable siren has me captured. I break the kiss and hesitate.

I am not sure I can be gentle. She looks down at me, sadness on her face. Uncertainty looms in the space and her eyes.

"What is it?" I look up at her.

Don't you know I will do anything you ask me to?

"Do you still find me attractive?" She points to her eye and the bruises on her legs.

Relief washes over me because a part of me thinks I am not worthy of a Siren like her. However, my heart breaks at the insecurities I created.

I sit next to her on the bed. She mistakenly interprets my reluctance as hesitation, but I am afraid of how I can be, and I don't trust myself to be gentle.

"*She Walks in Beauty* is a poem that reminds me of you," I say, holding her beside me and caressing her thighs. I want to scoop her in my lap, but I don't want to scare her with my more than sizable erection, eager to come out to play.

"You mention that your mom was an English teacher, and you read many literary works growing up." She rests her head on my shoulder. We both look at the pastel wallpaper that accents her fine silver dresser. "I had a brief glimpse at all the books in your library and was impressed." Her voice trails off. "What does the poem mean?"

I grin, happy she remembered my mother and my love for literature.

"Lord Byron's poem, *She Walks in Beauty*, compares a beautiful woman to a clear starry night. Her beauty marvels the heavens, but her virtue, peaceful mind, and loving heart walk with her even when no stars are in the sky."

Tears well up in her eyes. I knew she would have gotten emotional, but I wanted her to know how I *see* her.

"I am attracted to the beauty that one *can't* see, your strength, your determination, how you treat people when no one is looking, and how you don't give up. I am attracted to your purity and innocence. I hesitated because it scares me how attracted I am to you."

For further proof, I hold her hand and guide it, tracing parts of my back and shoulder. The parts of my body I backed away from her touch earlier.

She gasps. Her eyes widen in surprise. She quickly kneels behind me in the bed, examining the tattooed wings with black, gray, and white tattoos. She finds what I keep secret, what has been haunting me for over a decade.

"Gavin!" she screams as she traces the intricate wings of a fallen angel, clouds, skulls, and crosses. "The art is so vivid and realistic that it feels as if I can reach out and touch them, but they are covering..." she pauses and studies more. "They are *hiding* stitches and burns," she whispers and continues, her voice breaking. "But I see the artwork's beauty as parts of your body were transformed into a three-dimensional masterpiece."

I stand up to face her. There was a time when I hid the scars, the chemical burns, and the poison grafts they put in my skin. I rarely talk about them, not even to Alex and Duncan. *She is healing me.*

"The point is..." I scoop her up in my arms. "You don't find me less attractive, do you?"

She squeals. "I find you more attractive; you are a fucking badass, but seriously, what happened? Can I help somehow?" She searches my eyes while she holds my neck as I carry her bridal style down the hall and back to the hot tub.

Siren, you've helped more than you ever know.

"I guess we should talk some more in the hot tub. I will eat your sweet pussy later."

When I see her agape mouth at my declaration, I can't help but chuckle.

CHAPTER 21 – DEIDRA

"Though it was quite heavy, I found the strength to push through with the help of therapy and the support of my buddies, especially Cortez," Gavin says, taking a sip of wine as if he hadn't finished telling me about the months he spent in captivity being used as test subjects for skin and cell regrowth.

Sadness takes over the garden space as if the moonlight willed all creatures not to stir in observance of what Gavin just shared.

My hands grip the tub's seat, and the jets send cascades of waves over our bodies, causing Gavin to lean into a jet's water pressure and moan.

I fight back tears as the realization of what he went through and what he relived recently certainly might have put him on the edge.

"How is Cortez, is he…?" I ask, but I am reluctant to hear the answer.

"Cortez is in Arkansas. He inherited the family farm, and with his bionic legs, he manages well. I think he returned home for a girl he knew and couldn't forget, but he was responsible for saving my life, so I named my company after him." His eyes flutter as if he is recalling a painful memory. "We set up ten percent of the firm's revenue to donate to his foundation in Arkansas."

"What about the village girl, Ana?"

"Cortez's assistant to this day. She is in Arkansas with him."

"Did you?" I ask gingerly. "The women too?"

"Did I kill them?"

I nod. *He is justified, but killing women, I am not sure I am okay with.*

"I didn't," he stares off as if he is looking at ghosts. "I couldn't, not all of them; I couldn't kill the villagers. Cortez was right. Even at that moment trying to escape, rage consumed me, but because of how I was raised, mercy interjected..."

I release my breath with a long exhale. "Amazing." It is the only word that comes to my mind, but I want to say more. "I am sorry that happened to you," I cry out, tracing my finger over the ink number 0321 etched on his biceps.

We sit in silence with the night sky above—a soft sheen of condensation from the steam glistens on his face.

"I can't imagine what you went through looking for me," I breathe out.

He takes my finger from grazing over his biceps and kisses them. His silver eyes are like a wolf's stare, ready to pounce. I swallow hard as my body hums at the sight.

I don't mind being his prey.

"You know gray eyes are the rarest shade of eye colors." I went on to rant about eye color and the rarest to not-so-rarest, ranking them like a game show host.

Gavin chuckles, and his gray eyes darken. He gently pulls on the strings holding up my bikini top. The bright pink top falls to the water and floats in contrast to the white of the jets.

"You know, I may not know how many people there are with gray eyes in the world, but I know you ramble off facts when you are nervous." He grins.

My heartbeat speeds up, and my mouth goes dry. His stare is intense, and I am drawn in.

"I am going to take care of you. No need to be nervous," he whispers as his thumb takes turns grazing my pebbled nipples, which are getting more taut with his touch.

"Who me?" I tilt my head back. "You talk about nervous, and you are touching me at will, yet any time my hand reaches to touch you…" I make an exaggerated look down toward his dick, "Down there, you block me." I cover my breast but only punish myself because I already miss his touch.

"Well, I am not going to stop you," he says with a wicked smile, pulling me closer.

"But, you *are* stopping me. I mean, you are blocking me with your forearm," I reach down and grab.

"See, you are blocking me."

His eyes narrow. "Siren," he whispers with a sly smile and raises both hands. "That is not my forearm."

I cannot recall any time I have been so bashful.

I am witty and clever and can take anything that comes at me, but can I handle Gavin's anaconda?

As if he heard me. He scoops me up to face him. The Jacuzzi's jets whirl around us. Gavin sits on the edge of the tiled seat that circles the inside. He motions for me to wrap my leg around him, and I instantly oblige.

I stare into the wolf's eyes. My belly also feels like jets are whirling inside of it. If the outside whirling stops, I am sure he can hear the sound of how fast my heart beats.

"I know I am not strong enough to protect you," I say, through tears I keep at bay, "but I promise to keep you safe."

Silence fills the space, and he growls like a feral wolf in need, causing my nerves to get the best of me. He removes my pink bikini bottoms, the bikini bottoms that started this madness.

"You know wolves only mate once. They live the rest of their lives with only one mate," I offer him the news.

I push down my nerves and reach down to touch his rigid cock that is trapped in his boxers, only peering out at the slit in the crotch area... A battery of excitement heightens when I see his large dick bobbing back and forth in the water, circling like a shark seeking sustenance.

However, the wolf won't heed the shark's needs. In one swift move, he heralds me in the air and holds my hips up while he stands to his full length. He buries his tongue in my pussy. I instinctually wrap my legs around his shoulders and fists his dark, curly hair.

The pleasure is unmeasurable. His gray orbs lock on my gaze. I now know what the fairy tales meant when they say that time stands still. Not only time, but my heart is standing still. He teases my clit with kisses after putting his tongue *all the way* past my entrance.

He positions me like he is eating some juicy fruit, licking and sucking while lapping up all of my nectar, similar to how I eat a juicy mango.

"That's it, Siren, come all in my fucking mouth. Your pussy is getting claimed tonight," he says in a raspy, husky voice. He meets my stare and adds, "And forever."

Digesting the magnitude of his words, I nod in agreement as he continues to hold me, suck me, and kiss me. He is feasting like the wolf he is when he circles my clit with his tongue and gently sucks.

"Fuck," I scream. "Right there, right…"

There is no screaming. There are no words that I can form or can enter my mind. My mind is blank. Only bliss enters, and when my sanity returns, my screams follow. The orgasm I am experiencing is ecstasy at its finest.

I collapse into his arms as he catches me with the

cocky grin of his on full lips. My brain is telling my lungs to do their job. This man just took my breath from me. Now, I am struggling with basic intake and outtake of air.

Gavin carefully carries me out of the hot tub like I am some naive virgin he has to lay claim to, and I relish it.

CHAPTER 22 – GAVIN

Through the window, the moonlight catches her body, shining amber hues on her perfect, radiant brown skin. Her skin is so velvety soft that I am afraid to touch its delicate texture, making me humble by the privilege.

She is still in a daze from what I did to her in the hot tub. It was her fault; she was delicious, and I might have to feast on her later tonight. The mere act of touching her makes me feel like Basil in the novel The Painting of Dorian Gray. Basil was greatly fascinated by Dorian's beauty. A smile plays on my lips.

If my fate were like that of Basil, at least I would have had a night with the siren.

I question if I could feel love for someone so quickly. I am certain I feel more than love. I am *in love* with this woman.

"I know I am not strong enough to protect you, but I promise to keep you safe." Her words replay in my thoughts.

My thoughts are interrupted when the towel slips from my waist at an inopportune time. This foils my plan to linger and observe every part of her curves while drying her off with the fluffy towel.

Her mouth forms a wide circle as she gasps at my huge erection and backs away. However, she doesn't get far as I hold her right hand and intertwine our fingers, guiding her to sit on the bed with me. Defcon 4 alert is about how to control myself.

My cock wants to be inside her, and I can feel the ache down to my heavy balls. I haven't been able to make love in years. I fuck for pleasure and to keep the demons at bay. I want her, but I want to please her...

Be honest with her, be brave, and let her know what you want. I tell myself.

I start by clearing my throat. "The day we met, I went to the clubhouse to see you, but the pool party was over; mostly everyone was gone. However, I spotted you in front of the building; you were talking to Mr. Johnstone's wife."

"You were there when I was talking with Esmeralda?" She raises an eyebrow and leans in to hear more.

I nod, holding her hand, feeling the heat between us.

"I wanted to see you after we learned about all the threats your company faced. I couldn't hear you, but I saw how you made the woman feel better. You held her face and wiped away her tears." I say, not daring to look at her warm brown eyes. "At that moment, I felt something for you. Hell, it was lust when you bent down to pet Kevin," I chuckle, and she giggles. "But it became something more when I saw how caring you are."

Silence and suspense fill the air, and then a low giggle follows.

"The first time I saw you was while you were riding your motorcycle. You were riding without a helmet, and I thought you were a mirage."

"A mirage?" I ask.

"Yeah, I thought that there was no way men built like you lived in this neighborhood." She chuckles. "Then it turns out that you are the number one bachelor in Spring Ridge." She attempts another elbow but pulls back with realization when I protect my ribs.

Don't be a coward. Tell her what you want.

"Did you mean what you said the other night when we were on the sofa about how you feel when you see your sister interact with your nephew?" Fear about the subject I am bringing to her is found in the low tones of my voice.

The look of surprise on her face let me know she knew exactly what I was referring to.

"About having children?" She narrows her eyes. "I feel like I told you my life story that night, which turned into morning."

I nod. My Siren expressed that she had always wanted a big family but settled on doting on her nephew since she is about to turn 36 this year.

"Are you volunteering? To be the daddy?" she says with a wry smile.

"I am volunteering to be everything to you," I cup

her face. She is making this moment trite, but I need her to answer the ask. "Say yes. I am clean; I can show you my screening results. I want to enter you without protection..."

She cut me off. "Don't you care to know about me?" She exaggerates the words. "Results."

"Siren, I trust you with everything and anything."

She throws her head back and laughs. When she sobers up, she looks down at my cock, smiles, brings my hand to her face, and kisses it. "Caution be damn!"

She leans into me and kisses me, moaning into my mouth when I kiss her back, but if she continues this way, I won't be able to control myself. I will take her hard and fast. I decide it is in her best interest if I break the kiss.

I maneuver her to the center of her bed. Her body contrasts the peach-soft comforter. Gently I hover over and engulf her round, supple breast in my mouth, sucking her taut nipple while caressing the other breast. She moans as I part her folds and inserts two fingers in her dripping pussy, and she gyrates on them.

She is like puddy melting in my arms as I piston my fingers in her tight hole. She claws at my forearms as if she wants me to stop.

Seeing her eyes closed, I demand, "Look at me, Siren."

Her eyes open on command, and she arches her brow to show me she is still my bold siren. Her eyes are wild and expressive. *She is driving me mad.*

She sits up and moves her head to position her tongue to lick the piercing on my right nipple. My head goes back in pleasure as she holds the metal bar in her mouth and sucks hard, pulling with her teeth and then flicking it with her tongue while stroking my cock using the precum that has leaked as lubrication.

"I fantasized about doing this," she moans while sucking and grazing on my nipples while pulling on the bar.

"What the fuck are you doing?" I say, shuddering in pleasure. My voice is wild and feral.

She looks down at my pulsing erection, and with a seductive smile, she says, "I am not afraid of the big bad wolf."

CHAPTER 23 – DEIDRA

Did I just challenge the Wolf? I am brave, I am sexy, and I am...

"You should be very afraid," he exclaims, in a voice so gruff that it reverberates through my body and down to the core of my sex, almost onsetting an orgasm.

He peppers kisses on my neck, takes one hand, and holds both of mine above my head, pinning me. He licks my jawline, and with his other hand, he opens my leg, holding my right thigh open.

"Shit, Siren, you are so wet for me," he whispers as he caresses me, parting my folds to finish what he started. He continues to massage me, but I want him. I want more.

His weapon is aligned at my entrance, and I open myself for him, parting my legs wide. The want has become a need. *I need him inside me.*

"Please, baby, I want you," I mumble because I am losing my mind.

The things his fingers are doing to me are not enough.

He takes his painfully sweet time and puts the head of his monster dick in. I breathe, and his breath matches mine. *He is controlling himself.* I realize that his breath is labored. I act on my devilish thought to raise my body to meet his thick weapon; we must put ourselves out of misery.

He kisses me furiously. I moan in his mouth as he throws caution out the window and fills me up.

The pain is not slight, and I gasp at the action, but the pain goes away in seconds; the pleasure lingers as he stills himself inside me. His hip meets mine. His beautiful eyes assess mine as if he is observing if I can manage him. I nod, and he eases himself in and out.

The strokes are initially short but pick up long, fast, and powerful momentum.

It is like an itch I never knew existed and is finally being scratched.

The feeling of this man filling up every part of me is more than extensive. My stomach starts to constrict, and I lose myself. He lets me go as if he senses that I will need my arms. My hands automatically go to his tight butt, feeling him as he thrusts in and out of me, willing me to climax.

"Come for me, Siren," he says in a hoarse voice as he picks up the pace. When his silver gaze meets mine, I come undone.

Tears fall uncontrollably, and my body shudders as if I am in another dimension for at least seventy seconds —a dimension where bliss cannot be described with any scientific reasoning. The feeling is overwhelming and utterly beautiful.

I enter reality again to experience his kisses and

his moans. His voice is a guttural cry before he floods my pussy with his load.

I hold him tight as he peppers kisses on my wet cheek. I stay still, mesmerized by what is occurring.

"I love you and can imagine you in my arms forever," he says, catching me off guard and changing the mood.

My body stiffens at the magnitude of his words.

Did I give him the wrong idea? Yes, I want children, but love is too soon.

"Gavin," I say in a voice so serious that the vibe instantly changes. "I know. There is a pull between us, sort of a magnetic charge."

I stare into his eyes and ease my back to the headboard to rest in a sitting position. My eyes linger on him, admiring his muscular body and beads of perspiration sheen, highlighting every muscle.

He runs his finger up and down my arm. His face is pensive, and I can tell he is eager to hear what I have to say, but I stay quiet, not wanting the moment to be heavy with thoughts that I have yet to articulate.

His tone is low and pleading. "You are willing to have children with me because your clock is ticking, yet you don't want the full package: a home, marriage, family, and *love?*" His brows pinch as I sense he is trying to comprehend my logic.

He deserves an answer.

"But, Big guy, can we wait three to five months

before we call it anything?" I ask. "I watched my mother get caught up in the idea of love, and it unraveled her. I think love needs examination and consistency."

His eyes narrow. He opens his mouth to say something but doesn't when I interrupt.

"Please, I don't want to argue with you on this. Love needs to be consistent. Love is not a feeling; it is a choice."

He nods, and it is like he understands my thought process. Relief fills my senses because this is a boundary I am setting and not breaking, even though I know I love him.

"You might need five months, but I already know what it is. If you need five months, you got it, and I won't push," he adds.

He gets up, pulls me off the bed, and lifts me over his shoulder, caveman style.

"I shot loads of cum inside of you, so let's get you cleaned up," he blurts out.

I hit his arm. "You are so crass." I giggle.

"But you love me," he puts me down in the bathroom as he runs the bathwater.

He turns to face me with a questioning look as if he needs me to confirm the statement he just declared.

I give him a sly smile as I nod my head in confirmation.

Mr. Gavin Bright, you are mine. I will keep you safe

and never let you go.

CHAPTER 24 – GAVIN

Five months later…

The 6-carat engagement ring dangles under Kevin's neck, tied in a neat bow, and gleams underneath the bright lobby light of the exclusive Spring Ridge Clubhouse.

"We can do this right, Kevin boy," I exclaim to Kevin the cat. He gave me a husky meow to let me know he understood the assignment.

Duncan, Alex, and I sat in the hallway of the Clubhouse as Deidra led the HOA meeting.

"Damn, I never knew how long and painful these meetings are?" Duncan whines, fisting his fingers through his hair. "If I had known, I would have told you, you were on your own," he quips.

"If Deidra's nephew can stomach a two-hour meeting without complaining, that says a lot about you." Alex scolds Duncan. "And, if you bailed, Gav still has me and Cortez is on FaceTime."

"So, her sister is in there?" Duncan's eyes light up as he stands and peeps into the huge HOA makeshift ballroom for parties and meetings. "If she is as hot as her

Deidra, I want an intro."

Disappointed that all he could see was security smiling back at him and the back of heads, Duncan sat back in one of the leather seats lining the corridor.

Alex raises a brow. "She has a kid, remember. What happened to the motto: Women who have kids can't get any of the Duncan Special." He taps Duncan on the back and reminds him of his arrogance, saying that he doesn't mess with women with children.

"Hang tight, guys," I say while holding a struggling Kevin. I don't want to put him back in the carrier. "Irene just texted. Only ten more minutes."

"Cortez wanted me to FaceTime him during the moment, but he has been on standby for two hours now," Alex mutters while examining his phone dock near the wall outlet, charging.

As I look at my friends, all wearing suits and ties for me, I can't help but feel a sense of security and gratitude. Everyone Deidra and I love is in that room where she presides over the HOA company's board of directors meeting.

The day she met my mother was one of the happiest days of my life. They get along well. They are strong, beautiful women who believe they can do whatever they want.

Yeah, Momma Bright is a force. What she told me that night when I took her to the airport for her flight back home solidified my plans. *Boy, if you don't marry her soon and make me grandbabies before I get too old to spoil them, I will never speak to you again.*" I smile at the memory. Now, my momma is in that room waiting for me to enter.

Just about everyone knows I am proposing to my Siren today, and they are all here to share in the celebration. I knew I would propose the day she sat across from me in the conference room almost five months ago.

Even though our security firm is under investigation because everyone who was involved in my Siren's kidnapping miraculously disappeared, we are doing extremely well. The Gnosis software is literally changing the game in terms of identifying threats in the Security Sector.

I cannot confirm or deny what happened to the individuals who dared to kidnap and worry my soon-to-be wife. Let's put it this way: Duncan and I have been having fun over the last few months.

As if he knows I am thinking about him, Duncan eyes me and smiles, then waves at me as if to say, "You're welcome."

The smile is eerily similar to Deidra's nephew— Ben's smile. I shook my head. He can't be; it is a major coincidence, the eyes, the same first name. Siren never talks about Ben's father. When I investigated him, he was some dude in Colorado who divorced Bernie immediately after Ben was born. His lost. Ben is a great kid. *I can't wait to have children with my Siren.*

Memories take hold of me as they often do now— happy memories about my Siren.

"You know sirens are evil creatures in mythology," Deidra *whispered in my ears as I led her to the car after taking her to her favorite restaurant. I love dating her, taking her places, and showing her off. She added, "I looked up Homer and all the works about sirens; they lured sailors to their deaths." She sat in the truck with her hands folded, looking out the window and pouting.*

We pass through George Town, a quaint neighborhood in D.C., then to Downtown DC, where some of the nation's monuments serve as backdrops to the glorious night sky.

I sit, smiling, remembering what I said to my Siren.

"Maybe men are the evil creatures. They kill, pollute, lie, steal, and cheat. The sirens are the ones who protect nature from the creatures that they deem evil. I don't think of them as evil; I think of them as justice." I meet her gaze. The streetlight shows off her smooth brown skin and the beautiful glow of her eyes.

"Before I met you, I thought of the world of all these threats I can't control. I cared about fingerprints on fine marble and calculated every scenario before making a decision."

She interrupts. "You still do that."

I laugh and continue to grip the steering wheel, exposing my truth.

"To me, the world was like Defcon statuses, Defcon 1 to 5, in which I constantly calculated threats in my head. The day after we first slept together, my world changed. You killed the evil, Siren. You changed my life. You tamed me."

She reached for my hand and kisses it. "Tamed you?" She laughs loud in the car. "You are still feral and wild, but I like that. I love you, Gavin Martin Bright," she murmurs with a seductive smile.

The door to the party room opens, taking me out of my happy memories. Irene pokes her head out.

"They are wrapping up," Irene whispers, her eyes growing big behind her oversized frames. She looks at the fellas. "Damn, you guys look like you can be on a magazine cover." She blushes.

"It is time," I call out. I hold Kevin as I walk toward the door and then place him down in the room. "Run to Momma," I say, my heart beaming with anticipation when I get a glimpse of her in the middle of the row of desks, like a makeshift chamber flanked by a row of her fellow board members.

CHAPTER 25 – DEIDRA

I have presided over the HOA meeting as President for three months now, but for some reason, this meeting seems surreal.

Maybe the meeting seems surreal because of my anxiety about the several pregnancy kits I bought earlier in the week and have yet to take, hidden in the bottom of my purse, or maybe it's because of the unusual presence of my family and friends in attendance.

I like this part of the board meeting the most. It's when the HOA board members hear from the community members. The business part of the meeting lasted about two hours, and now it is time for the easy part, as we hear our residents' concerns.

Why did my sister insist on bringing Benjamin? The poor kid was patient, listening to music and playing games on her cellphone. Every once in a while, I winked at him to let him know I appreciated him being so good. I am grateful that Gavin likes hanging around with him. He looks up to Gavin, and my heart melts when I see them together.

Gavin will be a great father; I must stop procrastinating and take the test.

I push down the thought of the materials in my purse that could change the course of my already happy life with Gavin and smile at Bernie. My gaze then goes to Dorothy, Gavin's mom, who gives me an incredible, wide-tooth smile.

In fact, tonight, I just about winked and smiled at all the family members in the audience except for Gavin. My Big guy is working with the boys tonight.

Earlier this month, we received an official letter stating that Danvers Research Lab and Facilities would be an offered company on next year's stock exchange. We already celebrated, but it so happens that Irene decided to round up the girls for ladies' night since she stopped by the house to deliver the official SEC letter initially sent to the Austin office.

My sister has officially relocated from Austin and is staying at the house I gave her. She has been an incredible help as she works at the office to ensure the executives who relocated from Austin would find everything to their liking in the C Suites since I have been unexpectedly tired over the last few weeks.

I didn't want Gavin to worry, so I pretended to be okay because the last time I was sick, the big guy made me stay in bed while he waited on me hand and foot.

My father decided to stay in Austin and continue to lick his wounds from his failures. I think Bernie is more upset that he is a selfish jerk, but she tries to hide it.

Gavin's mom and Bernie insisted that we all go to the meeting when Irene persisted in saying that we should have ladies' night to celebrate because Gavin is working late tonight. Still, I would instead call it a night after the meeting and take the particular test that has been burning a hole in my purse all week.

Girls' Night is fun, but even one night away from Gavin makes me uneasy. My friends Carol and Esmeralda are also here. *Maybe I will invite them, then make an early exit.*

Carol and Esmerald have become like two peas in a pod ever since I introduced them to each other. I had to send them a stark look when I could hear their giggles during the meeting, during which they both pantomimed the word, *sorry.*

"Time is up!" The Vice President roars at Ms. Fitzgerald, an eighty-year-old neighbor who complains at every meeting, waking me from my thoughts. Ms. Fitzgerald's face holds a nasty scowl, and the room hums with whispers and chatter. However, there is another disturbance in the audience. Mumbles and laughter follow the crowd in the back of the room.

My eyes peer to the back of the room to see who is causing the commotion.

My heart almost leaps out of my chest when our beautiful orange cat, Kevin Trixie Bright, jumps on the table and flops before me. I move the table microphone out of the way to examine the huge sparkling diamond ring around his neck. My hands flew to my chest in surprise.

I heard his voice greeting the members before I could spot him. First, I saw Duncan's tall frame. Then, when I adjust my gaze to the left, I see my man. *My, Man.*

He wore a tailored-to-perfection navy pin-stripe suit with a crisp pink shirt, and his unruly curls were slicked back. *Damn, he looks good.* Alex is on his left, holding up a cell phone. I squint my eyes to see Oscar Cortez on FaceTime, grinning from ear to ear.

Duncan escorts me away from my seat to the center of the room. I never knew Ms. Fitzgerald's face could sport a smile, but I spot a broad smile on her face as Alex brings the item on Kevin's neck to Gavin.

My man gets on one bent knee and reaches in to take my left hand. I can already hear sobs in the room.

"Siren, from the moment you came into my life, it hasn't been the same. You make me want to be a better version of myself. You stun me not only with your looks but with your heart. You walk with such beauty. Ms. Danvers, you have so many titles in your life."

His voice cracks, and his fingers tremble as he reaches for the most stunning diamond ring I have ever seen.

"You are the CEO of your company, which is scheduled to be publicly traded. You are a loyal sister, a great aunt, a scientist, and President of the HOA." The room erupts in applause, but Duncan shushes them, and my baby continues. "Would you please consider giving me the honor of taking another title but forever?" Tears form in his eyes. "Please be *my* wife. Would you marry me?"

Tears blur my vision as I stare at the large ring. I answer through loud sobs. "Yes, only if you will be *my* husband."

Gavin puts the ring on me, picks me up, and swings me around the room to wild screams and applause.

His brothers, the Recon Marines, surround him as he holds me tight. "Siren, nothing can top this night," his loud laughter envelopes the room.

"Big guy," I whisper in his ear as he is about to put me down, "Wait, the night is not over; I have something to tell you."

CHAPTER 26 - GAVIN

This woman never ceases to amaze me. I wanted this evening to be special for her, but with the information she shared, I couldn't focus on our conversation at the restaurant I brought her to earlier. I reserved the whole restaurant for the evening and planned to seduce her during the meal.

I know she has been tired the last few weeks. I chalked it up to working hard to make the D.C. office successful. I eye her stomach. *Could she be?*

I couldn't wait for another second as we huddled in my Land Rover Defender parked next to her car at the community clubhouse, underneath a lamp post, about to look at six different pregnancy tests. I insisted that she go to the private restroom in the clubhouse to take after we pulled up to retrieve her car.

When she whispered the news in my ear like the Siren she was, my eyes went wide with excitement. I begged her to take all the tests in the bottom of her purse, including the ones I had just purchased.

"Why didn't you tell me?" I pry. *My stomach is tied up in knots, but I must be calm for her.*

"Because I wasn't sure, and you know you tend to

do the most." She stares at the six test kits lying on my console and the one I held in my hand.

I chuckle. Knowing that Deidra always wanted children and witnessing her relationship with her nephew, I prayed that we would have our own. I was willing to adopt if we couldn't have any.

The glow of the dashboard light flickers inside the vehicle, casting a warm hue on her face. *God, she is beautiful.*

"Gav, suppose…you know, they are not positive?" She frowns.

"Then, we will keep trying." I lean in to kiss her hand; the engagement ring serves as a reminder of my commitment.

The outside world is a blur as I wait with my Siren. "It's over three minutes. "Whatever it says, remember I love you, and we will face it together."

She nods and inhales. I breathe and peek at the small plastic stick I hold tight in my hand. Against the stark white background, the word "pregnant" was written.

"Two plus signs – and one reads pregnant; big guy, we are going to be parents," she screams through tears.

Tears bite at my eyes. "Siren, only you."

She picks up another stick, and her brows knit. "But this one says not pregnant," she states, disappointment shows on her face. "And this one doesn't show anything. What if…"

I don't wait for her to finish. I pick up my cell and dial Duncan.

"Please don't tell anyone until we verify," my Siren whispers.

I am sorry to disappoint her, but I have to know.

"Duncan," I say, my voice harsh. "I wouldn't ask if it wasn't urgent. This request will probably stump you, but if you can arrange it, please let me know. I need an official pregnancy test and a sonogram." I wait for him to digest my words before I add, "Now, tonight."

We sit in my truck, and Siren holds my hand tightly when Duncan calls back with the address of a well-renowned Gynecologist in the area.

"I'm sorry, baby. I can't wait; we must know officially, especially if you are okay," I whisper and start my truck.

She clasps her hands in front of her mouth and nods in agreement.

God, please make it true. Am I going to be a father? Please make it true for her.

CHAPTER 27 – DEIDRA

I steal glances at Gavin's wide grin as he drives up to the gate to enter the community. I know the news we just found out was too much to contain.

Gavin and I broke down in tears at the doctor's office when we received the news.

We wanted to bask in the bubble we created, just our family, for a bit longer. It was after midnight, and Gavin drove around for an hour.

I am four months pregnant, so I guess the little bloat is not a gluten allergy. Duncan called three times, and we shared the news with him and swore him to secrecy. I can't wait to tell Bernie.

"Why does Duncan have all these connections? More importantly, why do they do what he asks of them? After ten o'clock, Dr. O Malley agreed to see us; that is not normal," I ask my soon-to-be baby daddy.

He chuckles and ignores my question. He places a hand on my stomach when we reach a stop sign. "Twins, Siren. Twins?"

I nod and giggle, "I should have mentioned that the odds are in our favor, considering my mother is a twin." I smile and look at the sky as if she can see me. "I knew it deep down, but I was too afraid to receive confirmation in case I was wrong."

"I am so sorry," he whispers.

"About my uncle?" I ask.

He nods.

"I never met him, but I felt like I knew him from my pictures and how my mother often talked about him and my grandmother and grandfather. Especially him, they were super close."

Gavin knows about how my mother's family died when she was in high school. A tracker trailer took out her whole family on the way home from my uncle's football game.

"That is why my mother was so sad most of the time. She was obsessed with my father and wanted to be loved so much. Could you imagine loving someone so much it hurts?"

"I can." Gavin blurts out. "I am so sorry, honey."

My heart melts. I thought I was happy before. *This is happiness.*

Pulling up to the clubhouse again, I smile at my husband-to-be. He reaches in to kiss the palm of my hand, then slides out and runs to my side to open the door. He lifts me out of the truck, and I roll my eyes. *He is so dramatic.*

"We can leave my truck here and take your car home," Gavin instructs.

"Baby, I can drive home; there is no need," I explain.

I glimpse at the twitch in his jaw. I know there was no arguing with Gavin. Before, he was overprotective of me; I could only imagine how he would be with Babies on Board.

I roll my eyes and hand him the keys to my Lexus.

I am not in the mood to hear him lecture me about taking care of myself.

"Where's Kevin?" I ask with a giggle to throw him off; his stares are so intense. "He must be tired; he did a good job tonight."

"Mom took him home. She was tired as well."

"I haven't seen or heard from my sister and Benjamin since you proposed." I turn to him, standing on my tippy toes, and kiss him. "Thank you. This night was perfect."

He snakes a hand around my waist, shakes his head in disbelief, and kisses me. I sigh and slide into my car, feeling content and peaceful.

Gavin settles in the car and frowns. He presses the start-up button. "I meant to ask you about your sister's ex-husband because when I saw her in the party room earlier, she was all smiles. Then she saw Duncan, and the smile left her face."

"Oh?" I yawn. "Baby, the truth is my family made up the story about *her* ex-husband to save face because she was the heir apparent. My father was embarrassed to have her be involved in the company after she got pregnant."

He turns off the engine and turns in his seat to face me with wide eyes. "Who is Ben's father?"

"Bernie doesn't know his name or anything about him. It was a fling when she studied for her PhD in the Baltics."

"Fuck no." He turns to me with wider eyes than before. "*Duncan?*"

"I thought about it with the eye color and the way they both smile the same, but Bernie knows the father's first name only, and it's Benjamin, not Duncan."

"Duncan's first name *is* Benjamin. Ben Duncan. We call him Duncan. It's similar to Cortez. His first name is Oscar," he whisper yells.

"I never knew that," I whisper yell back and smack my hand on my forehead. "Wait a minute...is Duncan still staying at your guest house?"

He nods. "*Our* guest house," he corrects me. "He says he is leaving next week."

I might be the CEO of a soon-to-be publicly traded company, but Gavin and Alex's investments make my company look like small potatoes. The Gnosis Software applications have been taking off since Gavin invested in revolutionizing data and security applications that can be integrated with all military platforms. He and Alex are low-key, filthy wealthy. However, they keep their finances and company information very confidential. Earlier during dinner, I informed him I would agree to sign a prenup, and he scoffed at me even before he confirmed that I was indeed pregnant.

He starts the car to make the short drive back to his home, *I mean our home* since I gave my sister my house last month.

"Do you know where Duncan is going this time?" I ask.

"Duncan is a wild card; he does what he wants. Alex and I believe he is running from something, but I am reluctant to ask him." He shrugs with a frown.

When he pulls up in the long driveway, parks my car, and comes around to open the door for me. I hold him and cup his chin. Sometimes, I can't get over his rugged good looks.

"Big guy, promise me if Duncan is Ben's father, we won't interfere and let it cause friction between us," I ask my handsome fiancé. "I mean, I do not want anything to mess up what we have created."

"Siren, I was thinking the same thing."

He reaches in and kisses me. I deepen the kiss. My heart flutters as it often does when he lifts me out and carries me towards the house.

"Besides, something tells me Duncan is in for a whirlwind of a time." He gestures his head toward the lit pathway leading to the guest house.

Lo and behold, I see Kevin trotting down the path toward the guest house with a yellow scarf in his mouth.

I arch an eyebrow. "Yellow is my sister's favorite

color."

Our laughter echoes through the foyer when Gavin opens the door.

"Ms. Danvers, Siren, I love you and will spend the rest of my life showing you. You are right; love is a choice, and I choose to love and give you and our baby," his eyes dance as he corrects himself. "*Babies*, love every day."

I wrap my arms around my husband-to-be, the father of my children, and melt into him.

I am happy, grateful, and blessed.

Message from the Author, DJ Gunn:

I hope you enjoyed Deidra and Gavin's story. I had so much fun developing the characters, especially trying to convey how Deidra's determination to achieve her goals initially made her seem aloof and uncaring.

As a new author, I rely on readers to help this story find its audience. If you enjoyed this book, or can offer feedback, please consider leaving a short, honest review or rating. Your feedback not only supports me as a writer but also helps other readers discover stories they'll love.

Thank you for joining me on this journey. I can't wait to share what's next!

Are you excited to read about Bernadette and Duncan's story coming in the Spring of 2025? I am super excited to share it. I wonder what Benjamin Duncan is running from and how come he has so many connections at his beck and call. I love a good hidden baby story, especially from a guy who decreed that he does not want to have relationships with single mothers. Do you think Bernie will forgive her father for disowning her? Will she tell Duncan she took home a permanent souvenir from their fling in the Baltics?

It was ironic when Ben Duncan kept nagging Gavin about Diedra's sister, and between you and me, I was shocked to find out he more than knew her—he was the baby daddy.

I can hear Maury in the background saying, "Duncan, you are the father."

I can't wait for you all to read the next up in the series: Suits and Skins: The Sins of the Father.

To learn about upcoming books and novellas, please sign up for my newsletter at www. DJGunnwrites.com or email Deilia@djgunnwrites.com and type Sign up in the subject line.

Upcoming Releases:

"Written in the Skies"
"Hidden Among the Stars"
"Mommy Issues"
"Suits and Skins: Sins of the Father"
"Suits and Skins: Meant to be Wired"
"Suits and Skins: Rooted in Time"
"Made for Cyn"
"Daddy Issues"

ABOUT THE AUTHOR

Dj Gunn

I can write about my love of animals and growing up in Brooklyn, NY, and now living in the Washington, D.C., area, but to truly understand who I am fundamentally, here is a little insight into who I am.

A high school yearbook was my most treasured possession when I was graduating high school. I was turning 16, and most students were older than me.
I wanted to fit in and have their approval. I was somewhat popular, an athlete with excellent grades, and boy crazy, so when my father insisted on writing in my yearbook, I didn't want him to because I thought it wasn't what the cool kids were doing, but I couldn't refuse. You just don't say no to Jamaican parents.

My father not only wrote in my book, but it was like he took out a full-page ad on the back page. I rolled my eyes when I saw the verses of writings of G. Linnaeus Banks four-verse poem in my book, I Live for Those Who Love Me.

I was embarrassed, and my need to fit in with my peers outweighed the importance of what my father wrote.

I carefully tore out the page. I was a weak girl, but that experience taught me never to be weak again. The popular kids didn't really know me and sure didn't love or understand me like my father did.

My father is no longer physically with me in this world, but he knew who I was before I knew I was. I am a person with conviction. I am a mother, a business owner, and a great friend. Basically, I live for those who love me. Here is the last verse of the poem: my Daddy tried to instill in a lost 16-year-old girl who wanted everything from anyone but didn't realize she had so much more in front of her:

I live for those who love me,
For those who know me true,
For the Heaven that smiles above me,
And awaits my spirit, too.
For the wrong that needs resistance,
For the cause that lacks assistance,
For the future in the distance,
For the good that I can do.
For the dawning, in the distance,
And for the good that I can do.

I also love the outdoors and cats.

ACKNOWLEDGEMENT

Often, I have arranged people around me in columns, simple categories if you will, to guide me in knowing who I spend time with and gauge how they influence me. Still, everyone played a part in motivating me to write, so I wanted to send a special thanks to them:

The People in Column 1:
Those who genuinely love me and those who wished me well. Thank you for rooting for me and warmly encouraging me along my journey. I felt the love warming my thoughts as I wrote.

Those in Column 2:
Those who pretended to care and used what I offered freely but whispered negativity and doubts behind my back. Thank you for inspiring me to prove you wrong.

Those in Column 3
Those who spewed discourse and put up roadblocks, thank you for not wishing me well. You motivated me to dig in and finish these projects while the people in Column 1 broke all the spells cast.
Those in Columns 2 and 3 never stayed around me too long, but they were needed to teach lessons and grow my resolve. Reminding myself of the old cliché: There can

never be light without darkness.

Thanks to the Sunday Afternoon Writing Crew for inspiring me.

Finally, I want to send a special shout out to my editor, Tori Moore. Every incredible journey begins with the smallest steps. I was crawling along in the beginning, and she held my hands, guiding me to walk. With every step I take, I am filled with gratitude. Thank you.

If no one ever reads my works, the accomplishment of doing what I love is good enough.

Much Love,

DJ